What Folks Say About Steve Vernon

"WOW! BIGFOOT TRACKS is amazing. It's FUN but even more so, as some of the tales go way beyond just genre and are really moving and powerful as well. I would recommend this book to anyone who enjoys a good monster story." – Eric S. Brown, author of BIGFOOT WARS

"If Harlan Ellison, Richard Matheson and Robert Bloch had a three-way sex romp in a hot tub, and a team of scientists filtered out the water and mixed the leftover DNA into a test tube, the resulting genetic experiment would most likely grow up into Steve Vernon." – Bookgasm

"Steve Vernon is an anomaly in the world of horror literature. He's one of the freshest new voices in the genre although his career has spanned twenty years. Writing with rare swagger and confidence, Steve Vernon leads his readers through a gamut of emotions from outright fear and repulsion to pity and laughter." - Cemetery Dance

"Armed with a bizarre sense of humor and originality, a flair for risk-taking and a strong grasp of characterization - Steve's got the chops for sure." - Dark Discoveries

"Steve Vernon is a hard writer to pin down. And that's a good thing." – Dark Scribe Magazine

"This genre needs new blood and Steve Vernon is quite a transfusion." –Edward Lee, author of CREEKERS

"Steve Vernon is one of the finest new talents of horror and dark fiction" - Owl Goingback, author of CROTA

"Steve Vernon was born to write. He's the real deal and we're lucky to have him." - Richard Chizmar

Big Hairy Deal

A

Creep Squad

Novel

By

Steve Vernon

Stark Raven Press

2015

DEDICATION

I want to dedicate this novel to all of those writers, dreamers, and believers in Bigfoot. We all need a whole lot of dedication and I say this to you – it is far better to chase a dream than to run from your fears that the whole world might be laughing at you.

What the heck do they know, anyway?

Yours in storytelling,

Steve Vernon

Big Hairy Deal: A Bigfoot Novel
Author: Steve Vernon

ISBN-13 9781927765289

First Createspace Printing – June 20, 2015

"Fifty-eight percent of Canadians believe that Bigfoot exists while only 27 per cent believe in politician's promises at election time, according to a survey of 1000 Canadians conducted by Praxicus Public Strategies Inc. for the Canadian Taxpayers Federation" - Thursday, September 11, 2008 Metronews.ca
TORSTAR NEWS SERVICE

Chapter One – The Bear, the Bigfoot and Me

LET ME TELL you a story that is almost true and completely factual – except for the parts that REALLY count and them I mostly made up.

My name is Adam and I happen to have three Dads.

One of them is dead.

One of them isn't dead – but he isn't exactly alive, either.

And the third one is mostly mythical.

Like I said – a true story – and it happened something like this.

Just let me tell it to you.

One moment I was standing in the Cape Breton Highlands – and why in the heck did they call them highlands, anyways? I mean, they don't look all that high to me. Everywhere I look all I see are rocks and trees and rolling terrain and it seemed more of a humpy kind of a hill country rather than any sort of a highland.

I ought to know.

My Dad – my REAL Dad – has seen the Rocky Mountains and the Himalayas and from all of the stories that he hadn't had the time to tell me about all of those REAL mountains but my Mom told me anyways – I figure that those mountains my Dad saw were a heck of a lot "higher" than Cape Breton could ever dream of.

"This is Cape Breton Bigfoot country, Adam," Warren told me. "So you had better keep your eyes wide open."

That's Warren Teller talking – the guy who happened to marry my Mom, Penelope.

He met her on the highway. Mom's car had a flat tire and he had pulled over and offered to help fix it – which would have been a really nice thing to do if he had ACTUALLY known how to fix the tire. It turned out Mom had to tell him how to do it and he still goofed it up along the way.

The man was a moron, in my opinion.

Worse yet was the way that Warren was ALWAYS trying to tell me all of these long and stupid stories that had absolutely no point at all - about mysteriously unidentified flying saucers and deep sea underwater monsters and more boring old ghost stories than you could rattle a rusty set of leg irons at.

As far as I was concerned Warren must have somehow substituted a pot full of boiled asparagus in place of his brains, somewhere along the way. In fact I am pretty sure that the doctor dropped him on his head at birth. In fact I am ONE HUNDRED PERCENT sure that after that doctor had picked baby Warren back up from the delivery room floor Warren's mother had most likely dropped him back down again two or three times just to be sure that he bounced all right.

Warren is actually my stepdad – which is another way of saying that he was a bit of a total complete and freaking dork.

I mean just take a look at the guy. He is built about as thin as a green reed with a lumpy Adam's apple that sticks out from the skinny of his neck and bobbles up and down like he was constantly trying to swallow a live kicking bullfrog inside of his throat.

The man looked absolutely one hundred percent gorky.

There just wasn't any other sort of a word for it.

In fact – if you look up the word "gorky" in any dictionary that you care to mention I bet you ten bottles of ice cold orange pop that you will see a picture of Warren, skinny neck and all – still swallowing that bullfrog.

"But Adam," my Mom would always tell me. "He is your stepdad, after all. You are just going to have to learn to get along with him."

"I don't have to get along with him if I don't want to."

"Well," Mom would always tell me after I said that. "If you cannot get along with him you'd at least better learn to listen to him."

Which always got me angry.

"I don't have to listen to ANYBODY!" was how those sorts of discussions usually wound up ending with – that and a slammed door.

There was just no way around it.

I knew what Warren really thought of me – even if he didn't know it himself. I was the kid of some other guy. I was in the way. I was something to be put up with. The way I saw it Warren mostly wanted my Mom all to himself and I was just some kind of an unnecessary detail that he would have gladly loved to sweep under the carpet with last month's pizza crumbs.

I didn't care what he said differently.

As far as I was concerned – all that Warren being my stepdad actually meant was that he had accidentally married my mother about six months after my real Dad was accidentally killed by that unexpected baby carriage.

Which sucked.

My real Dad getting killed happened about six months ago outside of a little Afghanistan town that was called by a name that sounded like someone's mouth was full when they had named the town what they did.

Do you want me to tell you just exactly what killed my real Dad?

An I.E.D. was what they called it in the newspaper – an improvised explosive device – and I cannot tell you just how many times I have wondered about what other kinds of words you can spell with those three little letters.

I.E.D.

Just what was that supposed to freaking mean, anyway?

Why don't they just call it what it really was?

It was a stolen baby carriage filled with four cooking oil tins full of high explosive and a case of roofing nails.

So that's exactly what I would call it.

I would call it a B.C.F.W.F.C.O.T.F.O.H.E.

And a case of freaking roofing nails.

Who would do something like that?

Who would even think of such an idea?

I mean, what did he do – get up one morning, eat himself a peanut butter and banana and honey sandwich and then say – hey, today I think that I am going to build a bomb out of a baby carriage and maybe blow somebody's Dad up with it?

Now that is a question to chew over.

Never mind talking about freaking Bigfoots.

"There is no such thing as a Cape Breton Bigfoot," I said back at Warren, only half-listening to what he was trying to tell me. "They are totally made-up and mythical."

That is me – Adam Sawyer – wearing that Batman backpack that my mother bought me in a Halifax Wal-Mart, hunchbacked on my shoulders so high that I looked a little like somebody really ought to have named me Wild Bill Quasimodo.

"It's a true story," Warren said. "I read it in a book."

I didn't mind stories.

I just hated people telling them to me all the time. I mean, if I wanted to hear a story I could turn on the television or check out Youtube or even read a book. I just hated having to listen to somebody going on about something that probably didn't ever happen the way that they said it did.

I hated English class for the very same reason.

"Don't believe everything that you read," I told Warren.

And I left it at that.

My Batman backpack was WAY too gorky for a seventeen year old kid like me to wear – but my Mom had bought it for me – so I cut her some slack and I wore it whenever I didn't think anyone else was actually looking.

I cut my Mom an AWFUL lot of slack these days – except when it came to Warren.

I just had NO patience for the man.

"It's true," Warren repeated. "The story goes that over the last century there have been many reported sightings of a gigantic humanoid with long shaggy fur prowling through the forests of the Cape Breton Highlands."

Holy gorky squared infinity plus.

What was this moron trying to tell me?

Warren was telling me that like he was reading and reciting it off of a blackboard scrawled in boring-colored chalk in the boring-part cortex of the left-most boring side of his brain.

"Sure," I said. "And there are just as many reported sightings of kids enjoying themselves in the middle of a pop math quiz – but that doesn't really mean that it's true."

"It's true," Warren said for the third time – as if saying a lie three times was going to make it stick any closer to the facts. "The local folk call him the Cape Breton Bigfoot. Early pioneers first spotted what they described as an eight foot tall ape-like beast with a tangle of snarled dirty hair and a pair of car-door-stuck-out ears and what most people described as the most soulful pair of large brown eyes that you could ever imagine."

Wonk-wonk-wonk-wonk-wonk, blah!

"Really?" I asked. "Did early Cape Breton pioneers REALLY HONESTLY describe him as having car-door-stuck-out ears?"

"That's a metaphor," Warren said. "I was just being colorful."

"You want to be colorful," I said. "You ought to try bathing in red and green paint – the checkered kind. You could probably pick yourself up a can or two in the How-Stupid-Can-You-Really-Be store."

"Very funny," Warren said. "It's a true story whether you giggle at it or not."

I just rolled my eyes sarcastically.

"It sounds to me like that particular story has long outlived its best-before date," I pointed out. "Which in my mind makes it the worst kind of green and blue molded-over baloney."

I don't know why Warren was acting so upset about what I was saying to him. I mean, I was just trying to set the man straight. It wasn't like I was calling him a liar or a dork or a doofus – now was it?

"The story is true," Warren repeated. "As true as story can be."

"And where did you hear that?" I asked.

"Stories are everywhere," Warren said. "Heck, these hills are FULL of stories just begging to be told."

What a laugh.

"Sure they are," I said, sarcastically. "I bet you there are whole caves crammed full of stories. I bet you there are caves just puking stories out of their mouths like the kid who ate too much birthday cake."

"I bet there is," Warren said. "You keep your eyes open and you might even just see it."

"I bet there is not!" I replied. "It is stupid and it is dumb and I don't believe in your stupid dumb stories."

That second stupid and dumb seemed to hurt Warren's feelings.

"That hurt my feelings," Warren confirmed. "Don't you even believe in anything? Don't you even believe in monsters?"

I thought about what Warren was asking me.

I thought about that nameless guy sitting over in that unpronounceable village in Afghanistan – chewing on a mouthful of peanut butter and banana and honey sandwich while visions of exploding baby carriage bombs rolled and boomed through his head.

I thought about that very same guy sitting over there and giggling as he carefully packed that box full of roofing nails into the baby carriage full of high explosive.

So, yeah – I believe in monsters.

Only I didn't tell Warren any of that.

I just stood there and I stared as he bobble-swallowed another giant bullfrog in the back of his long skinny throat.

"No Warren," I said. "I don't believe in monsters and I don't believe in Santa Claus and I don't believe in the Tooth Fairy and I sure as Wikipedia don't believe in any sort of Cape Breton Bigfoot. There is nothing out here in these woods except maybe a couple of lost wandering grizzly bears."

I folded my arms on my chest to show him that I meant business.

"Cape Breton is too far east for grizzly bears," Warren said, shaking his head and giving me that look of his that always seemed to say to me – my golly, just how stupid can one kid get. "The worst thing we might come across is a cranky black bear or else maybe a coyote – and both of those animals are pretty shy of humans."

It turned out that Warren was more right than he actually knew.

In fact, he was absolutely right about grizzly bears not being in Cape Breton and I knew it myself because I had already looked it up on Google before the hiking trip, just in case – but I sure wasn't going to tell him that.

According to Google, Cape Breton Island was an island on the northeast end of Nova Scotia that measured about ten thousand square kilometers in total – making it the 77th largest island in the world – or Canada's eighteenth largest island – and what kind of a brag was that, really?

We're number eighteen so we try harder?

Big hairy deal!

The highlands actually were the tail end of the North American Appalachian Mountains – and according to some geologists Cape Breton originally was physically connected to present-day Scotland and had only been separated by a couple of million years-worth of continental drift.

It's true.

I looked it up on the internet – and the internet NEVER lies.

"We're perfectly safe," Warren concluded. "No grizzly bears, no mountain lions, not even any dinosaurs. No sir, there is nothing out there but the possibility of a rare and random unexpected Bigfoot sighting."

I know that he was just trying to make me have something close to a good time out here but I wasn't going to let him get away with it.

"What-freaking-ever," I said, fishing my I-pod ear plugs out and squishing them just as deep into my ears as they went.

Warren shook his head like I had said something pitiful and sad.

Then he started to softly sing.

"Bigfoot went over the mountain, Bigfoot went over the mountain."

I'm not saying he was any good at his singing.

I mean, talk about pitiful and sad and gorky to the ultimate max!

The man couldn't carry a tune in a cast-iron bucket if you glued the bucket handle into his grip.

"Bigfoot went over the mountain," Warren sang, badly off key. "Bigfoot went over the mountain. Bigfoot went over the mou-ount-tain, to see what he could see."

I knew what he was doing. He was just trying to make me laugh and forget about my grumpiness but I was not going to fall for that.

I held onto my frown like it was piece of Bigfoot-proof armor.

There was no way that I was going to let him see me grin.

I jammed my earplugs even deeper into my ears.

I touched a button.

Somewhere deep inside of my two year old i-pod my favorite band – The Squealing Sacred Sea Monkeys – began shrieking out my absolute favorite song – Misunderstood #23.

We are talking fifteen minutes of raw electric guitars, jackhammers, bagpipes and three guys yelling MISUNDERSTOOD-NUMBER-TWENTY-THREE, MISUNDERSTOOD-NUMBER-TWENTY-THREE, MISUNDERSTOOD-NUMBER-TWENTY-THREE.

Which was just plain absolutely perfect for drowning out a stepdad's off-key singing.

Next, I bent a stick of peppermint gum into my mouth and I started chewing just as loudly as possible.

Warren hated loud chewing. He complained at every meal – telling me to close my mouth because he said that I sounded like an animal. And then I would say that I needed to keep my mouth open to breathe while I chewed and then Warren would blow his own breath out in a display of exasperation and then Mom would tell me to listen to my Dad and then I would listen to my Mom and I would pretend for just a little while longer to listen to Warren – who really wasn't my for real Dad.

Baby carriage or not.

Which is why we were hiking out here in the highlands of Cape Breton.

We were out here because Mom had some sort of freaking convention to go to and Warren had decided that he and I really needed to bond. That was the word he used. Not bond, like in James Bond – but bond, like in glue.

That word "bond" always made me laugh. It made me picture the two of us – Warren and me, stuck together in a tangle of Crazy Glue, Quick Dry Cement and leftover boiled oatmeal after the pot had dried on the counter overnight.

I am talking gross.

Warren said that he and I really needed to get on a hiking trip together and that we would bond like a real stepdad and stepson ought to – an idea that was lame enough to need its own wheelchair ramp and a handicapped parking permit and maybe even an extra set of crutches and a cast.

I mean, I could be sitting in a Toronto movie theatre right now – eating a big old bag full of salted popcorn and chewing on a well-ketchuped hotdog.

Heck, I could have even been watching a movie in a Halifax theatre – which was about as close to being in Toronto as a single green pea was close to being a forty acre field of pea plants – but I wished that I was there and not anywhere but where I really was – namely, here.

With Warren.

I swatted at a mosquito – which was a little like draining one eye dropper's worth of sea water out of the bottom of the Atlantic Ocean. The bugs out here were thick enough to eat a grown kid alive. I absolutely hated being up here in the Cape Breton highlands. As far as I was concerned we were way too close to the clouds. I had the feeling that the sky was going to open up and swallow whatever was left of me after the bugs got through with chewing their fill of my flesh.

I missed television.

I missed movies.

I missed candy stores.

And I missed Dad.

But for now – all that I could do was to look straight ahead and try my very best to ignore Warren's off-key singing.

"Bigfoot went over the mountain."

The man didn't give up easy, I'll say that much for him.

We kept on walking.

There was a birch tree standing about twenty feet in front of us – with that pale white bark that birch trees wear, tattering loose from the tree's trunk like a paper jam in a printer.

I focused on that birch tree.

I told myself that so long as I kept on walking towards that birch tree that everything was going to be just fine.

Then something strange happened.

The bark of the birch tree began to blur and ripple and twist. Then the bark grew oddly furry and then the tree grew into a bear.

I know just how that sounds.

I know that the bear must have actually been hiding behind that tree only it sure did not look that way to me at all. It looked more like there was some kind of a door hidden in that tree – a door that the bear just stepped out of.

And that bear looked freaking mean.

You know how you always see bears in the movies and they either look cute or kind of gawkish and clumsy?

Well, this here bear was neither cute nor gawkishly clumsy. This here bear was a Godzilla-sized grizzly bear – about one thousand pounds of stink and claw and tooth and ugly stomach hunger that was going to kill us and eat us and he did not seem too particular about the order in which he was going to accomplish this in.

Warren was right.

There were no grizzly bears in Cape Breton.

But I guess this particular grizzly bear did not know that.

I guess that this grizzly bear maybe had not studied his geography.

In any case, that badly-misplaced grizzly bear charged straight directly at us.

"You have to tell," Warren quietly said – looking directly at me as he turned to face the charging birch tree grizzly bear.

I have to tell what?

Warren didn't say anything else.

All that he did was to stand there and wait.

I saw Warren put one hand up towards that oncoming birch tree grizzly bear, as if to say stop. The grizzly bear swarmed over Warren's skinny stuck-out arm like he was a big gigantic furry tidal wave. The next thing I knew Warren was lying on his back on the ground being eaten alive by that gigantic birch tree grizzly bear.

I mean – how do you deal with something like that?

This bear was eating my freaking stepdad – a guy that I hated – but he was still my freaking stepdad – and more importantly, as skinny as Warren was he might just not be enough to fill the hunger of a for real birch tree grizzly bear.

I opened my mouth to scream.

The stick of gum that I was chewing on slid down my chin and it stuck there like a chunk of peppermint-flavored fungus.

The Squealing Sacred Sea Monkeys kept on shrieking MISUNDERSTOOD #23.

And all the while that birch tree grizzly bear had Warren pinned down in the dirt just chewing like Warren was a peppermint flavored meatball.

Warren still had that one skinny arm of his stuck straight up with his thumb jammed halfway into the hollow of the big bear's ear. It looked as if he might have been rooting for ear wax. I don't really think that Warren's thumb was hurting that birch tree grizzly bear all that much. The bear had his head pushed down into Warren's windbreaker and the t-shirt underneath and was gnawing and chewing on what was underneath the t-shirt.

Namely, Warren.

I ought to do something.

I ought to pick up a rock or a branch and charge in there and rescue my stepdad.

I ought to show that birch tree grizzly bear that my kung-fu was a whole lot stronger than all of his stink and his hair and his teeth – only I did not have any sort of kung-fu and that birch tree bear was awfully freaking big.

I couldn't do a thing. It was like I had been zapped with an alien paralysis ray.

I was frozen stuck with fear.

The only thing that wasn't frozen stuck was my mouth. My mouth was open and it was screaming louder than a hundred horror movies rolled into one.

Which was right about when the Cape Breton Bigfoot showed up.

For real – and totally un-mythological.

<u>Chapter Two – Pure Harmonized Terror</u>

UP UNTIL THIS moment I had thought that the Cape Breton Bigfoot – or for that matter any sort of Bigfoot-type creature in the whole wide world - was nothing more than a figment of somebody else's sick and twisted imagination - but I guess that the stories all were true because here he stood – almost tall enough to stunt double as a totem pole with arms that dangled somewhere close to his anklebones and feet that looked big enough to snowshoe clear to Alaska on them if he wanted to.

That Cape Breton Bigfoot was running straight down the side of the hill, straight at me – and then he spread his arms wide and then he flew.

Or at least that's what it looked like to me.

Halfway through mid-charge Bigfoot tripped one big left foot over a teetered-up rock. Then he flipped over and stuck that same big left foot up into the air behind himself in the wrong direction and pointed his nose straight down towards the dirt and sort of cart wheeled face-first straight down the side of the mountain.

I'm not saying it was pretty.

Mind you that birch tree grizzly bear was awfully surprised to see that Bigfoot coming, like he was. The birch tree-bear let go of Warren who sort of lay there in the dirt and bled quietly. I couldn't tell if Warren was breathing or dying or just lying there dead already.

As for me, I was still frozen stuck with fear.

The birch tree grizzly bear stepped over what was left of my stepdad and stepped up towards Bigfoot who was still cart wheeling straight down the mountain.

Straight towards me.

The only problem being that I was stuck standing between the hurtling Bigfoot and the geographically-displaced birch tree grizzly bear – which was a really bad place for any sort of seventeen year old boy to be – especially if he ever dreamed of living to see eighteen.

So I ran straight towards Warren.

I believed that if I could get there to Warren I might either save him or maybe just hide behind him. At the same time I screamed even louder. I don't know if my screaming somehow helped my running much but it sure took my mind from off of my mad blind panic.

The birch tree grizzly bear came straight at me. All I heard was snarl. All I saw was teeth. All I could feel was fear. Do you want me to use bigger words? Do you want me to tell you how I was terrified and my heart was beating like a riot of heavy metal drummers? Forget it. I didn't have time for fancy description.

I was way too busy being just plain scared.

Meanwhile, that Cape Breton Bigfoot crashed into a pine tree. It looked like he broke his neck and a few other less important bones. The tree snapped in two and Bigfoot turned twice more times in the air. He hurtled over my head and then he smacked down back-end-first into the dirt with a mighty big thud.

I don't know about you – but I was pretty sure that the Cape Breton Bigfoot had just killed himself.

Which only left me with the Godzilla-sized geographically-displaced birch tree grizzly bear to worry about – so I supposed I ought to be grateful only I was too busy screaming. I was certain to run out of scream sooner or later but my vocal cords kept seeking out new octaves of panic. The Squealing Sacred Sea Monkeys kept screaming in my ears - MISUNDERSTOOD-NUMBER-TWENTY-THREE, MISUNDERSTOOD-NUMBER-

TWENTY-THREE, MISUNDERSTOOD-NUMBER-TWENTY-THREE and we were all making one heck of a noise.

I caught hold of Warren and I tried to drag him clear of the battle. I wasn't exactly sure where I was going to drag him to. It wasn't as if I had thought all that carefully about my next step. I just knew that I had to do something.

Like maybe get myself eaten alive by a grizzly bear that hadn't bothered to study his geography too hard.

I shook Warren.

He rolled his gaze up towards me. It looked to me like he was looking at me and through me and straight on past me. It looked as if he were trying to tell me a story with his eyes – like he was trying to stare out an entire forty-eight volume encyclopedia of meaning with one single momentary wide-eyed glance.

What was he trying to tell me?

I couldn't tell you, even if I knew.

Warren groaned a little. His t-shirt looked like he had accidentally dumped an entire pot full of homemade chili-con-carne right on top of it.

The only problem was I knew just what that chili-con-carne really was.

It was Warren's blood mixed together with pieces of Warren's grizzly-torn body.

Right now, Warren looked as if a dozen exploding baby carriages had gone off around him. He felt kind of wet and loose beneath the fabric of his t-shirt. I didn't know what to do about it. So I screamed again. Screaming hadn't helped me all that much so far, but perhaps the third time would be luckier than the first two tries.

And then the Cape Breton Bigfoot sat up and growled along with my screaming. I think he might have been trying to harmonize along with my terror and The Squealing Sacred Sea Monkeys - only he was going to have to do a whole lot better than he was doing in order to keep up with the likes of my kind of pure intense shrieking terror. I was screaming notes that would have given a rap-ranting opera singer a case of rusty-throated laryngitis.

The birch tree grizzly bear ignored my screaming and lumbered directly towards Bigfoot.

I would have been smart to run, right about then. Only I was way too busy screaming to think of any really smart thoughts. I should have thought of something else to do, like maybe peeing in my pants or learning to speak Lithuanian - but right now all I could think of was that if I screamed loudly enough then maybe somebody might actually hear me getting suddenly eaten to death.

At least then I could hope for a decent sort of burial, assuming the birch bear left anything behind to bury.

The birch tree grizzly bear got a little closer to Bigfoot. Then Bigfoot sat up a little straighter. Then Bigfoot blinked and he shook his head. He was drooling a little down one side of his chin and his eyes were wobbling – he had hit the ground that hard – but I wasn't about to pass him a napkin or a pair of corrective glasses.

By now that birch tree grizzly bear was making those angry hungry woofing choof-choof sounds that I had heard grizzly bears make on the Wild Outdoors Channel. Only I couldn't quite seem to be able to reach the remote control to change the channel – namely, because this wasn't the Wild Outdoors Channel.

This was a real honest to grizzly bear life and death.

Most likely mine.

Meanwhile Bigfoot raised himself up on the palms of his hands. He pushed himself upwards hard and then he launched himself forward in a sort of hopeful leaning leap, right at the same time as that grizzly bear charged on in.

Bigfoot had hold of a chunk of that tree trunk that he'd knocked down. I didn't remember seeing him pick that tree trunk up. I think it even surprised him that he was still holding onto it I guess it was just something his right hand did while he was trying to stand up. He swung that chunk of pine trunk at the birch tree grizzly bear, connecting with a fat wet smacking sound as the swung trunk landed square against the side of the grizzly's ugly wedged head.

WHACK!!!

The birch tree grizzly bear shook his head. He made another choof-choof sound and he kept on coming. Bigfoot reached his free hand straight out and he caught hold of the grizzly's thick woolly throat, figuring on choking the grizzly to death as near as I could figure. The grizzly reached out its teeth and caught hold of Bigfoot's stretched out forearm. Bigfoot swung the chunk of trunk down just as hard as he could on the back of the big bear's neck – three or four times in a row - which looked to me to be a big mistake.

The chunk of trunk shattered against the large hump of muscle on the back of the grizzly bear's neck. The next thing I knew Bigfoot was holding nothing but a fistful of sawdust, toothpicks and semi-ambitious splinters.

The bear reared up and caught hold of Bigfoot – hanging onto his slab like shoulders as if he was hoping for a fast lesson in slow dance technique.

The two of them looked like a couple of fat hairy and world-class-ugly television wrestlers, way too tired to go one more round.

So they just leaned on each other really hard.

It was an absolute deadlock.

Which was right about the exact moment that the coyote fell out of the sky.

I guess things happen fast here in Cape Breton.

Especially when you didn't want them to.

Chapter Three – A Big Shaggy Funny-smelling Eagle

THE COYOTE FELL out of the sky like somebody had accidentally dropped him from off of the top of a lonely wandering rain cloud.

All right – so I know just what that sounds like when I say it - but I had already witnessed a grizzly bear stepping out from the inside of a birch tree and I had seen an up-to-this-point mythical Cape Breton Bigfoot performing a triple-face-first-belly-flop down a Nova Scotia mountain side. Seeing a sky-diving coyote drop down onto a birch tree grizzly bear from off of a random wandering cloud didn't really surprise me in the least.

The coyote was about the size of a large German shepherd and he landed directly upon Bigfoot who had just finished landing upon the grizzly bear. The tri-multaneous impact of the coyote banging against the Bigfoot who banged upon the grizzly bear's back shook the ground around me like a small-to-medium earthquake.

"Woof," I said, as if the coyote had actually dropped onto me - only it sounded more like I was trying my very best to woof just like a grizzly bear. I wondered if somehow maybe I had actually said something in grizzly – like maybe please don't eat me.

At least I had managed to stop screaming along the way.

Bigfoot tipped backwards. The bear stood up and the coyote sort of shook his own head like it might have rattled inside.

Warren moaned just a little.

I wiggled the backpack from off of my shoulders, pulled off my windbreaker and tried to wrap it over Warren's chest like a big neon blue bandage – which only resulted in me getting some of Warren's chili-con-carne blood on my jacket.

Warren was dying.

There wasn't any other word for it.

I wondered if that was how it happened with my real Dad. It didn't much for me to think of me seeing him lying there next to that baby carriage on some dusty Afghanistan road, his blood and his vital fluids chili-con-carne soaking down into the dirt. I felt something wet quivering in the corner of my eyes and I told myself it was nothing more than a drop of chili-con-carne juice.

Meanwhile, Bigfoot did his best to roll and curl up and protect his own belly. Actually, it looked to me like he wanted to curl up into a big shaggy Boy Scout knot and maybe pull himself tight enough to somehow disappear up his own behind-hole.

Which didn't quite work.

The coyote stumbled over to the birch tree and leaned on it like he was slowly falling asleep. I think he might even have peed on the tree just a little too, which was kind of gross and probably smelled a little funny – even from this far away.

While all that was happening that wandering rain cloud that the Coyote had fallen off of seemed to sort of drift down out of the sky and park itself in a nearby thicket of alders – which seemed like a sort of a strange behavior for ANY sort of a rain cloud.

Then, while I was staring at the rain cloud, Bigfoot got one of his great big feet worked up into the gut of that birch tree grizzly bear – like he was trying to balance that big bear atop of one big foot. The next thing I knew Bigfoot twisted, trying hard to keep those big grizzly bear claws away from his rib cage – which had target written all over it. Meanwhile, the grizzly bear was doing his very best to swallow Bigfoot's entire left arm from the elbow on up. And then Bigfoot worked his other big foot up into the grizzly bear's big saggy gut.

I could see what was coming next.

"Do it," I said, whispering softly aloud to myself. "Get that big foot up there and kick-stomp old King Kong Yogi right back to the heart of Jellystone Park."

I'm not sure just when I had started to cheer for Bigfoot.

I mean, he was most likely going to eat me for dessert if he managed to make a main course out of the grizzly bear. I should have been crawling over to my stepdad and thinking about some sort of an escape plan - but my feet had still somehow not quite remembered how to move.

"Do it," I repeated. "Kick-stomp Yogi."

I still don't really know why I was cheering.

Maybe I had just watched one too many wrestling matches on television but I felt I had to root for somebody – and so far Bigfoot hadn't tried to eat me.

"Go, Bigfoot, go!" I called out.

The coyote giggled.

Now I didn't know that coyotes could giggle but then again I also didn't know that coyotes could sky-dive either. Meanwhile, Bigfoot threw me a dirty stop-bugging-me kind of look as if he somehow understood just exactly what I was saying.

Then Bigfoot pushed just as hard as he could with both of his big feet, his free arm, and the arm that the grizzly had almost swallowed nearly up to his elbow. He pushed hard, using all of his leverage, and then he flung that birch tree grizzly bear up off him. The bear made a fine fat arc across the skyline like a big shaggy funny-smelling eagle.

Then the bear sort of bounced two or three times hard when he landed and kept on rolling downhill. I guess being built on a slope the way he was – with his big high butt and his low-slung head he had a whole lot of trouble rolling downhill fast.

When he finally stopped rolling the grizzly bear picked himself up, shook it all out and did his very best to look as if he had intended all along to allow that Bigfoot to boot his big furry butt down the side of the mountain - which was right about when the coyote stood up, sucked in his breath and then he swelled himself up with a single mighty inhale. It was like he took a deep breath that kept on getting deeper.

He swelled himself up to about the size of a small-to-medium pickup truck birthday balloon and then he leaped – howling like a rabid fire engine siren – aimed directly at the grizzly.

At that exact moment, while the pickup-sized-coyote was hovering above the grizzly bear like a giant coyote-shaped hot air balloon in some sort of a weird Thanksgiving Day parade - a huge raven – about the size of full grown nuclear jet plane – swooped down and plucked the grizzly bear up like he weighed nothing more than a feather or two.

That raven beat his big black wings and then he took off airborne.

Only he didn't exactly pick up that grizzly bear.

It was more like the raven's claws reached down inside the bear's body and pulled out a living breathing thundercloud – which should not be confused with the thundercloud that the coyote had sky-dove from off of. I could see that tiny little birch bear thundercloud floating and hanging in the raven's grasp as the big bird beat its heavy black wings and disappeared over the horizon – thundercloud and all.

"Moose turds," Bigfoot growled – which I am guessing was Bigfoot for swearing.

Then Bigfoot bent down and picked up a rock the size of a Volkswagen engine and he threw it at the escaping raven – only he missed.

The rock knocked down an entire good-sized chunk of that alder thicket, almost crushing that rain cloud – so I guess that Bigfeet were environmentally unfriendly.

"Hey, watch where you go throwing them rocks!" a voice rumbled from somewhere deep inside of that alder thicket. "You nearly hit me that time."

I looked hard but I couldn't see anyone in there – unless maybe they were hiding there inside of that rain cloud.

Meanwhile, the raven flew directly over my head. I felt the raven's shadow pass over me and it was like one of those chills that came at you out of nowhere, running up and down your backbone like an army of frozen tap-dancing zombie-ants.

What was left of the grizzly bear just lay there and the coyote landed in the dirt right directly beside the bear's remains like a half-ton of awkward.

He made a sound like a falling pancake when he hit the dirt.

SPLAT!!!

We had won, I guess.

"YAY BIGFOOT!" I shouted out.

I couldn't help but feeling happy. If someone had given me a pair of bright pink cheerleading pom-poms I would have shook them hard and maybe done a triple-cartwheel and followed up with a double-hernia-split. It felt a little better than screaming, I supposed, but I still have had better ideas in my time. The way I figured it this Bigfoot was either going to eat me or save me for later – like maybe for a midnight snack.

I figured if I cheered loudly enough it might spoil his appetite.

What the heck - if worse came to worse I could always wake Warren up and get him to sing about going over the mountain again.

Maybe even on-key.

Bigfoot lumbered over towards me. It was a little like watching a fully grown wood lot suddenly up-root itself and take a casual sort of Sunday stroll. I could feel his natural Sasquatch heat and I could smell his stink and his heavy feet thumping down on the mountain side like a wall full of walking thunder.

I tried to run but somebody had nailed my feet down into the dirt.

Bigfoot got closer.

I looked around for someone to help. Warren just lay there and bled a little longer. He sort of bounced softly every time Bigfoot took a step. Warren was still moaning each time he bounced so I guessed he was going to live just long enough to serve as the second course in a two course Bigfoot banquet.

The next thing I knew Bigfoot was standing over me, his shadow nearly swallowing me whole. That was something to be thankful for, I guess. At least I wasn't going to die sunburned. So I opened up my mouth. Then I closed it again while Bigfoot stood over me just looking. Finally I found a few last words hidden in the dry and empty cave of my mouth, somewhere back in behind the pizza-stained enamel of my second left molar.

"Please don't eat me, Mister Bigfoot," I said. "I'm sorry I thought you were mythical."

Which really wasn't much as last words went.

Bigfoot blew his breath out through his lips.

For just a moment in time he sounded just exactly like my stepdad Warren, blowing his breath over his lips to show just how much teenage suffering he had to put up with. And Warren was right – the Bigfoot had a pair of the saddest-looking eyes I had ever seen.

"Eat you?" Bigfoot said. "Not even with a pair of rented-out teeth,"

I just lay there in the dirt and gawked.

Somehow hearing Bigfoot talk like that was even harder to believe then seeing him beat up on a way-out-of-place grizzly bear.

"And I for sure aren't no stinking myth," Bigfoot rumbled, before turning back to staring towards that fast-disappearing raven. "Don't think that I didn't hear you saying that earlier, loud and clear."

I still couldn't find anything else to do but stare stupidly upwards at something that was NOT an hallucination, a lie, or a rural myth..

"He doesn't really like to be called mythical," the Coyote said, leaning over me and grinning ear to fuzzy ear. "Just so that you'd know."

I nodded slowly.

Then I pinched myself.

"This isn't any kind of a dream," Bigfoot growled, without even bothering to look down at what I was doing. "So you can stop pinching yourself."

All the same I pinched myself again.

Which hurt.

Chapter Four – Talking With Bigfoot

I FELT MY jaw drop open. In fact I was fairly certain that my entire lower jaw bone had fallen off of my face and hit the ground and bounced about two or three times. After which I made a bah-bah-bah sound like a sheep with a serious case of jelly-mouth stutter.

"Bah-bah-bah-bigfoots don't talk," I stammered out.

"In the first place it's Bigfeet or Sasquatch - not Bigfoots," Bigfoot said. "Or do those weird plastic wires sticking out of your ears make it that hard for you to hear?"

"Bigfeet isn't very proper, grammatically speaking," the Coyote pointed out.

"Who asked you?" Bigfoot retorted. "And don't you be bringing your grandmother into this particular discussion."

"I said grammar," the Coyote snapped back. "Not grandmother."

"Actually, the word that you said was grammatically, not grandmother." Bigfoot said, following it up with a big wise-guy yellow-toothed grin. "Maybe I ought to check your ears to see if any of those weird plastic wires are growing out of them."

Weird plastic wires?

By now I had totally forgotten that I was still wearing my i-pod wire earplugs – which didn't help any attempt at inter-species communication much.

"What are you listening to anyway?" Bigfoot asked, rudely yanking out one of my earplugs with one big hairy hand.

Bigfoot jammed the earplug into one of his big hairy ears. My grandfather used to have hairy ears, but this guy had an entire South American rain forest sprouting behind and within each of his ears. He listened to the sound of the Screaming Sea

Monkeys for a moment and then made a face like he had just dry-swallowed a whole mouthful of unbuttered broccoli.

"What is this horrible noise?" he asked. "Don't you have any Johnny Cash tunes?"

Johnny Cash?

"No Merle Haggard? No Jim Reeves? No Hank Snow?" Bigfoot went on. "Don't you even have any freaking Willy Nelson?"

Willy freaking Nelson?

I guess a fellow can learn something new every day.

I had just now learned that the Cape Breton Bigfoot – mythological or not - had absolutely no taste in any kind of music.

"You can't be real," I told him. "I must have fallen and bumped my head. I must be hallucinating this whole thing. I am going to wake up in a hospital bed and maybe some pretty nurse will bring me some vanilla ice cream in a bowl."

Bigfoot just looked at me with a sort of how-stupid-can-you-get sort of expression on his big hairy face.

"You are still hung up on that whole mythology foolishness, aren't you?" Bigfoot asked. "You keep thinking this isn't real, don't you?"

I nodded.

"Let me tell you a little bit about mythology," Bigfoot said.

I moved my head up and down in what I thought looked something like a nod. I mean – who was I to argue with a nine foot tall Sasquatch?

"If you look that word *mythical* up in a dictionary you are going to read that a myth is nothing more than a traditional or invented or legendary story that usually concerns some being or hero or event – with or without a determinable basis of fact or a natural explanation – especially one that is concerned with deities or demigods and that explains some practice, rite or phenomenon of nature – such as WHERE DOES THUNDER COME FROM?" Bigfoot explained. "Do you got it?"

I nodded.

"That is a nice definition," the Coyote said. "Did you practice that much?"

"Every morning in front of the bathroom mirror," Bigfoot said. "It pays to be ready. There's just no telling when SOMEBODY is going to ask you a very stupid question."

I just kept on nodding hoping that I would wake up soon.

I think my neck muscles might have seized up on over-nod.

"Did you ever hear anybody tell a story called Butterhead?" Bigfoot asked me.

I shook my head no. It felt strangely good to me after all of that nodding.

"Let me tell it to you, then," Bigfoot said – and then before I could nod or shake my head he started in on telling it.

"This boy was visiting his Auntie and she gave him a piece of cake to take on home to his Momma. So he took that piece of cake in his fist and he carried it on home and by the time he got home the cake was fist-squeezed down to nothing but a handful of crumbs."

Coyote laughed at that.

"That isn't no way to carry cake, the boy's Momma told him. The next time your Auntie gives you some to carry home you ought to wrap it up in some clean leaves and carry it home under your hat."

"Hadn't he ever heard of a cake box?" I asked.

"Isn't the point," Bigfoot said – and then he got back to telling. "Come the next week Auntie gave the boy a pound of fresh, sweet butter to take home for his Momma and he wrapped that butter in some clean leaves and carried it on home under his hat but by the time he got on home the butter had melted and run down the boy's forehead, nose and chin."

"I hate it when that happens," Coyote added.

"That isn't no way to carry butter, the boy's Momma said. The next time your Auntie gives you some butter to carry home you ought to cool it in a clear flowing stream before you go trying to carry it."

A part of me wanted to ask Bigfoot just how he figured you could soak a pound of butter in a cool running stream and another part of me wanted to ask just what this story had to do with anything at all but he kept on talking and telling way too fast for me to get so much as a thought wedged in around his storytelling.

"Come the next week Auntie gave the boy a cat to take to his Momma, who was trouble with rats, so the boy took the cat on down to the stream and tried cooling it but that didn't work out too well and by the time the boy got home he was all scratched and tore up and his Momma laughed at him and said that the next time his Auntie gave him something to carry he ought to tie a little string around its neck and let it walk on home."

"Yeah," Coyote said, with a twist of a grin. "Just picture trying to walk a cat with a string. That'd work out really well."

"Come the next week Auntie gave the boy a loaf of bread to carry on home to his Momma to eat so he tied a piece of string to the loaf of bread and he dragged it on home and by the time he got home it wasn't fit for a cat to eat and his Momma just shook her head in disgust and said that she wasn't going to waste her time giving him any more sort of advice but that she had left six fat mincemeat pies cooling on the back steps and the boy ought to be careful about stepping in those pies so the boy walked on out back and he stepped in the middle of EACH of those six fat mincemeat pies one after another, just like his Momma had told him to."

"So what does that have to do with anything at all?" I finally had to ask.

"It's a story," Bigfoot said. "Which is another word for a myth. Boys are ALWAYS not listening and not thinking and goofing things up and that's all that the story is about – the way that it is easy for a boy or anybody at all to get the wrong idea from not listening and thinking hard enough."

I still could not get it and I told Bigfoot so.

"Just try and think of it this way," Bigfoot said, returning his attention to me. "A myth is nothing more than a lie that someone tells you when you are too young or too stupid to really know the difference."

I gave him one more nod.

"Usually, we can lay the blame squarely on the parents," Bigfoot went on, kneeling down beside what was left of Warren. "So is this your Dad?"

I wasn't going to let that pass.

"He's not my Dad," I said. "He's just my stepdad."

"Does that mean I can step on him?" Bigfoot asked. "I washed my feet last week and I even used soap on one of them."

I thought about that.

"No," I said. "It just means that he married my Mom after my real Dad had to go."

"So why did your real Dad have to go when he had to go?" Bigfoot asked.

I thought about that too.

The truth of it was Dad and Mom had gone off in completely different directions a l-o-n-g time before the baby carriage bomb had ever gone off.

That's all that Mom ever said about it – she just told me that her and Dad had both gone in different ways – like a good Boy Scout compass or maybe even a GPS or a good map would have kept the two of them together.

Now I am seventeen years old and I know fully well what the word d-i-v-o-r-c-e means – only Mom never ever used that word. As far as she was concerned she and Dad had just gone their separate ways – like he'd lost his way and just wandered off.

"I'm not sure, I guess," I said to Bigfoot. "All I know is that Warren took Mom to a dance and step on her foot so hard that he fractured it."

It was true.

Mom had to wear a cast for six weeks after. Warren spent the whole time at our house bringing her cups of tea and cooking her meals and cleaning the house and apologizing. It darned near drove me crazy listening to him go on about how sorry he was.

Worse yet, the only thing the man knew how to cook were grilled cheese sandwiches.

I don't think that I can ever stare another slice of processed cheese in the face if I live to be a thousand years old.

"You're not actually sure about that, then?" Bigfoot asked. "Are you?"

"I was awfully young when it happened," I explained. "But I always figured that it was my Mom's idea."

"But you don't really know for sure."

I did not.

"It doesn't matter anyway," I said. "My real Dad is dead now."

"You're sure about that too, are you?" Bigfoot asked.

I wasn't exactly certain what he meant by that – whether he meant that I wasn't sure about it not mattering, or if I wasn't sure about why Mom and Dad had divorced in their own separate ways – or if he had meant something completely entirely different.

But I would remember that question for some time to come.

"Ah well. Stepdad or Dad, it's all the same difference to me," Bigfoot said, tearing what was left of Warren's windbreaker from off of his chili-con-carne chest. "He still looks to be hurt pretty bad right now. Stepping on him MIGHT actually be an improvement."

"Pretty bad?" I repeated slowly. "Warren?"

I didn't know what to do or say. Here was my stepdad, the guy I supposedly hated, with his chest torn up so badly that it looked like he was wearing a bowl of chili-con-carne for a shirt. I ought to be Christmas-Day-happy but for some reason I couldn't seem to muddle past surprise algebra pop-quiz-glum.

Bigfoot leaned down close enough to breathe on Warren's wounds.

All I could see was a whole mouth full of teeth.

Oh my god.

He was going to eat my stepdad right there in front of me.

"Do you have any moss?" Bigfoot asked.

"Moss?"

I wondered if he needed the moss to make himself a salad to go along with all of this people-meat – which got me to thinking about the way that Mom was always after me and Warren eating salad with our meals. She always said that salad was good for our cholesterol – so maybe Cape Breton Bigfeet worried about their cholesterol levels.

"What are you, an echo chamber?" Bigfoot asked, reaching over and yanking some moss from the foot of a nearby tree. "You know, MOSS – the green stuff that grows on trees. Why don't you see if you can find some moss and maybe some cobwebs in that alder thicket. There ought to be some dew glinting on the cobwebs this time of the morning. Just look for the shimmer and you'll be fine."

I got up and ran to the alders he was pointing at. It happened to be the very same alder bush thicket that rain cloud that the coyote had jumped off of had landed in.

I could see the alder bushes just fine.

I could even see the shimmer that Bigfoot told me I'd see.

What I couldn't see was just why I was doing exactly what Bigfoot told me to do – except that maybe doing anything felt better than me doing nothing at all.

So I ran into the alders.

Now – for those of you who don't know quite what an alder is I can tell you that an alder is basically a sort of a weed tree. An alder will sprout pretty anywhere it wants to and just as soon as it sprouts up it begins to spread into big old thickets that will fill in the gaps where the trees left off and they'll choke out the younger trees. They're not really much good for anything but getting in the way of things.

I ran into those alders and I hit that alder thicket like it was a solid brick wall.

I'm telling you it hurt – and it did not make one single bit of sense.

I mean, all that I could see in front of me was just sticks and branches but I flattened out against it like somebody had parked a nine-mile-high planet-wide car in the middle of that alder thicket and I had run smack flat dab against the car door.

I fell flat on my back and when I looked up Bigfoot and the Coyote were both standing over me and laughing. Bigfoot was carrying what was left of Warren in his arms like he was nothing more than a little baby.

"That'll teach you to call me mythical," Bigfoot said, with a low rumbling chuckle that would have drowned out any avalanche you care to name.

I just lay there and groaned a little while the earth continued to spin in both directions at once.

And then the mystic pink Winnebago showed up.

Right out of thin blue air.

Chapter Five – Winnebago Alder Bush Surprise

I LAY THERE in the dirt, flat on my back, looking up at the sky.

A bird flew overhead. It might have been a crow. I wasn't certain – but I'm pretty sure that particular bird was looking down and laughing at me.

I guess I couldn't blame him much for laughing, if he was.

I must have looked pretty funny laying there by that patch of alders that I had just run into like they were some kind of a freaking brick wall.

"Didn't anybody ever teach you to stop and open the door before you go running into an alder thicket?" the coyote asked.

Door?

I sat up slowly, like my butt and my legs had been glued to the dirt and was refusing to go along with that whole getting-up part of things. The coyote reached down one paw and helped me to my feet.

I felt just a little surprised at how soft the coyote's paw really was.

"Upsidaisy," the coyote said.

I stood up twice as slowly.

Right about now I did not figure there was any need to rush into ANYTHING.

I took a good long look at the coyote that had helped me to my feet – but I couldn't really figure out just exactly what he looked like. He looked a little like a plain ordinary coyote – which I had seen in a couple of nature programs that my Mom had made me watch. At the same time he looked a little like that coyote that kept chasing after that roadrunner in all of those cartoon shows that I used to watch – back when I was a kid – three or four years ago.

At the same time I could see something else looking out at me from that whole mess of coyote and cartoon character – something that looked like a very old and very young Indian warrior – the kind you might see in an old western movie, only way older than movies.

"You can come out now, Winnie," Bigfoot said.

Winnie?

Like the bear?

Was he talking about The House at Pooh Corners and all of that kiddy-book jazz?

Or was Bigfoot talking to the ghost of the dead bear?

I was seriously confused.

"Are you sure that it is safe?" a voice asked from somewhere inside the alders. "That kid sure smells awfully funny to me."

"I'll vouch for him," Bigfoot said.

"Big hairy deal," the voice from the alders said. "You talk as if you are some kind of a fountain of Solomon-like wisdom and judgment. It just so happens that I have seen you chew the chewing gum that you find stuck to the bottom of park benches."

Bigfoot shrugged.

"Pre-chewed is way tastier," Bigfoot said in mid-shrug. "I like to think of it as my own version of environmental recycling."

"There is just no accounting for Sasquatch taste, I guess," the alder bush went on. "Or the lack thereof."

Bigfoot shrugged again.

On second thought – shrug was just way too small of a word to use on such a heavy gesture. It was a little like watching a mountain giving birth to an earthquake in the middle of a full-blown tornado.

"The kid is a souvenir," Bigfoot said. "Some folks bring home baseball bats and silver teaspoons and t-shirts. Me, I collect kids."

"That still doesn't mean I want him anywhere inside of me," the voice from the alders said.

Inside?

I didn't like the sound of that at all.

Being fed to an alder bush might be worse than being eaten by a Bigfoot.

"He's been touched by the Raven," Bigfoot said – and I could somehow hear him using that big capital R in Raven. "He's been marked. That means that he's our business now."

Then a door opened up in the middle of the alders – just the same way as that bear had stepped out of the birch tree.

The door swung open like someone was opening it for us.

And then all of a sudden like instant magic I could see this bright salmon pink Winnebago motor home – something about the size of Wisconsin that had been parked here in the alder thicket all along – maybe hiding in that coyote-dropping rain cloud.

Except that giant pink Winnebago hadn't been there a minute ago.

There was no way on earth that I wouldn't have seen it if HAD been here.

It was freaking huge and it was pink all-over – but other than that it looked exactly like one of those gigantic road-boats that you see prowling up and down the highway, usually driven by nine-hundred year old men wearing way-too-flowery Hawaiian shirts.

That is, except for the wings.

The big pink magic Winnebago had a huge pair of bright pink wings.

"A flying Winnebago?" I asked.

"Do you like them?" the Winnebago asked, giving those big giant pink wings a thunderous flap. "An eagle gave them to me."

"You mean , you won them in a poker match with a hand of five aces," Bigfoot corrected. "The only reason you got to keep them is that eagle never learned to count."

Then he looked back at me.

"Listen kid, why don't you step into my office?" Bigfoot said.

"Yes sir, Mister Bigfoot," I stammered.

"Why don't you just go ahead and drop the Mister bit, would you?" Bigfoot said. "You can just call me Bigfoot."

So I dropped the Mister bit and I stepped inside the magic pink Winnebago.

The Winnebago was even bigger inside than it had looked outside. I had the feeling like I had stepped into one of those big old manor houses – like the kind that Bruce Wayne would live in when he wasn't busy being the Batman.

There were rooms and there was a staircase and a shiny chrome fire pole that slid down to somewhere and a big old skylight that looked to be looking out at the rings of Saturn and I'm pretty sure that door in the wall lead to an elevator.

"Let me introduce you to somebody, kid," Bigfoot said. "This here is the third member of our team. He likes to be called the Prophet."

"Which is what his people called him back before he passed on over to the other side," the Coyote said. "Although I should tell you that it isn't his real name. The Prophet is just a name that he gave himself."

"Old Winnie has ALWAYS had a heck of a knack for spinning his own PR campaign," Bigfoot said.

I was still trying to get my head wrapped around the idea of a haunted travel home.

"You mean this alder bush is the ghost of a dead Winnebago?" I asked.

"A dead Shawnee, if you want to be specific about it," The Prophet – also known as the Winnebago said. "I am Tenskwatawa, brother to Tecumseh. I am Lalawethika – He Who Makes a Loud Noise. I am the Open Door and I am the Bringer and I am the Sender."

Hearing those words spoken from inside of the Winnebago felt a little like bit like I was hearing his voice speaking out loud from inside of my head – like somebody had planted an amplified speaker just left of my cerebrum.

In a way, hearing it like that helped me get over the idea that this was nothing more than a dream. The way I saw it, I had NEVER dreamed as loud as this – so I figured that what I was experiencing had to be the truth.

Either that or I had lost my mind.

"The Prophet has got more names than a Toronto phonebook," Bigfoot said. "But I mostly like to call him Winnie – short for Winnebago."

The Prophet made his displeasure known by puffing a small cloud of funky green smoke from out of his tailpipe.

I was pretty certain that he wasn't one bit happy with the nickname "Winnie" but I guess he wasn't about to argue with a nine foot tall Bigfoot beast.

"The Prophet was the brother to Tecumseh," Coyote explained. "Way back in the days of what some folks like to call the War of 1812. When he passed over the Great Spirit decided he was worth hanging to and so he brought him back in the form of Winnebago travel home – which only goes to show that the Manitou has a heck of lot better sense of humor than most folks give him credit for."

"This is a Pawnee travel home," the Prophet rumbled. "I don't care one bit what it happens to accidentally say on my bumper sticker."

There it was again. I could hear him talking like he was talking through my i-pod after someone had jammed the ear phones about three inches past the inner-end of my ear drums.

I must have winced, because Coyote DEFINITELY noticed me flinching.

"It will give you a bit of a headache at first, listening to the Prophet talk from this close up," the Coyote said. "But you'll get used to it. Ear wax helps, if you let it build up long enough."

Only I didn't want to get used to anything.

"I don't want to stay here," I said, taking two steps backwards. "I want to go home."

"This is your home for now, kid," Bigfoot said, laying Warren out on a table. "You're staying whether you like it or not."

Which almost sounded like some kind of a threat to me – and I guess coming from a nine-foot tall Sasquatch I had to treat it as such.

"You'll get used to it," the Coyote repeated.

"What's the matter with this one?" The Prophet asked.

A bright pink spotlight lit up around what was left of Warren.

"This one is that one's step-dad," Bigfoot said, pointing at Warren. "Only that doesn't mean that you can step on him. This step-dad has been bit pretty badly by a Spirit Bear."

"So who called the Spirit Bear?" The Prophet asked. "They don't come unless they are told to. Somebody had to have been pulling the strings of that ursoid, the way I see it."

"What's an ursoid?" I asked the Coyote.

"That's just another name for the Spirit Bear," Coyote replied.

"As near as I can figure the spirit bear was walking for Raven," Bigfoot theorized. "And I am pretty sure that Raven took a piece of this kid's stepdad with him when he left."

"Is that the dead guy?" The Prophet asked. "The stepdad, I mean?"

Dead?

"He's not dead," Bigfoot replied. "Not quite, anyway. Do you think that you can hold him on to his side of the curtain?"

"I can try," The Prophet said. "It will take a heavy weaving, but if anyone can do it, I can – for I am Tenskwatawa, brother to Tecumseh. I am Lalawethika – He Who Makes a Loud Noise. I am the Open Door and I am the Bringer and I am the Sender."

"Right, Winnie," Bigfoot replied. "Just do it, would you – and spare us all the reading of the resume. You make up half of that stuff anyway."

"Some of it is true," The Prophet asserted. "The best kinds of stories are made up out of little bits of truth stretched into a pleasing shape."

"So what are you doing to my stepdad?" I asked, interrupting.

I still couldn't figure out why I was so concerned about what was happening to Warren – but there it was.

I actually had feelings for Warren, dork or not.

"I thought you said that you didn't care about him," Bigfoot said.

"I didn't say that," I said, even though I really had said it.

"Winnie is going to hold your step-dad onto our side of the curtain," Bigfoot explained. "Otherwise he is apt to pass over."

"Do you mean die?"

"He means pass over," Coyote explained. "Dying isn't nearly as serious or permanent as everyone tells you it is."

"It isn't any more serious than leaves turning colors on an autumn tree," Bigfoot explained. "The leaves might fall off but the tree goes on living."

"If you say so," I replied.

If dying meant leaves turning color than I pretty sure that it looked to me as if Warren had a terminal case of autumn – and winter was close behind.

"And if we let him pass over with only half a spirit – and that's all that the Raven left him with," Bigfoot went on. "Then he'll slip into the darkness and be gone forever – which is a lot more serious than just passing away."

"You mean die," I repeated. "Warren is going to die, isn't he?"

"Something worse than just die," Bigfoot said. "But we're going to fix things – because fixing things is what we do best."

"Do it, Winnie," Bigfoot said to The Prophet.

I watched as a slow cocoon began to weave itself about Warren's body. The cocoon was made out of pine needles and moss and dead leaves and dirt and moth wings and fireflies and bull rushes. I could see all those things coming together from out of the nearby wilderness and weaving themselves about what was left of my stepfather's body until he looked like something that might have been found on the bottom of a swamp.

I touched the side of the Warren-cocoon. It felt warm and I could feel the warmth of the pine needles and dirt and rock moss and moth wings breathing beneath my touch. I could see something glowing deep inside of the Warren-cocoon – like the memory of a birthday candle burning somewhere in behind the dream of a cake crumb.

"That'll hold him, for a while," Bigfoot said. "But we're going to need to track the Raven down to get back what he took from your stepfather."

"Is he alive?" I asked. "My stepdad, I mean."

"He is," Coyote replied.

"For now," Bigfoot added.

For now?

"Can you do it? Can you help him?" I asked. "Can you actually fix him? Can you save my stepdad?"

I was scared and worried and it felt like maybe ten kinds of weird, worrying about Warren this way.

I thought I had it all figured out but I guess I didn't.

"Now don't be so worried," Bigfoot said. "Death isn't anything but a doorway. You can step in through it and you can step back out – and it hardly hurts at all. I remember dying once and it took me an awful long time to get back. You see, what happened is…"

"I don't care what happened!" I yelled. "Can you fix my stepdad?"

I still couldn't figure out WHY all of a sudden I was so all-fired worried about what happened to Warren – but I was.

"That's what we do best," Coyote said. "Fixing things."

"Fixing and saving," Bigfoot added. "That's our job. But you really ought to hear that story of mine. It's an awfully interesting tale."

"I don't want to hear any stupid stories," I said. "I want you to fix my stepdad."

"It's a pretty good story," Bigfoot said. "You really don't know what you're missing."

"What I'm missing is HOME," I said, loudly. "I want to go home, right now. I want you to fix my stepdad and then you can take me home."

"Nope," Bigfoot said, shaking his head. "You need to stay with us. You see, when that Raven took that part of your stepdad's spirit he took part of yours, too."

"You've been touched by the Raven's shadow," Coyote said. "Which means that if we don't fix this situation fast than you and he are most likely going to die."

That didn't help much.

"Die, or worse," Bigfoot added. "Like I said, there are a WHOLE lot worse things out there than just dying."

That helped even less.

But I guess beggars can't be choosers.

Especially beggars who'd been touched by a raven.

The light that was hiding in the heart of the Warren-cocoon that had used to be my step-dad glowed just a little in agreement.

"So what should we do?" Coyote asked.

"What do you think we ought to do?" Bigfoot replied. "It's time to call in the boss. If anybody knows what to do it would be the ghost of Sam Steele."

Which made about as much sense to me as anything else had the whole day long.

Chapter Six – The Ghost of Sam Steele

BIGFOOT STEPPED OUT of the pink mystical motor home with the slow, heavy and hairy majesty of seven unshaven gunslingers stepping into a High Noon street.

He took three steps forward.

I saw his eyes glaze over like he was squinting hard into some sort of middle-distance sandstorm trying hard to focus on something that wasn't really there.

He leaned back and opened his mouth wide enough to swallow a medium sized steam roller. Then he took a deep breath and yelled about as loud of a yell as was humanly possible for a nine foot tall Sasquatch.

"Hey BOSSSSSS!!!"

The trees shook just a little.

Maybe I did too.

"Loud, isn't he?" Coyote asked.

"Don't you have some sort of a radio or a cell phone that you could use?" I asked Coyote. "Yelling like that seems awfully undignified."

It was hard on the ears, too.

"Sure we've got a radio – or at the very least we've got SOMETHING almost like a radio." Coyote said. "In fact, we've got nearly everything that we need - but the big guy likes this way better. He says that the yelling helps him to think clearly."

Only by now he had stopped yelling and was just standing there and staring out into the forest as if he thought something was about to come walking out from the shadows.

And then all at once something did.

"I'm never sure if I hate seeing him walking out like that or love it," Coyote said. "But it sure is hard to forget – once you've seen it happen."

I could understand why.

A long tall figure came walking slowly out of the woods. It was a little like he had just stepped out of the tree bark and the foliage – in almost the same way as the Spirit Bear had stepped out of the birch tree – only this was a little slower like he was wading out of the deep end of a swimming pool full of pitch black midnight.

"Yes sir," Coyote said. "It is pretty nearly unforgettable once you've seen it."

He was one of the tallest men that I had ever seen. Not NBA tall, you understand. It was more in the way that he held himself. He had a sort of strength and a presence and a quiet kind of dignity – something like a preacher crossed with a WWE professional wrestler and a twelve man SWAT team, with a heavy helping of John Wayne thrown into the mix. He was wearing an old-fashioned Canadian Mountie uniform that looked about a hundred years old with a tall black fur hat that added about another twelve and a half feet to his altitude. He had a heavy cavalry-style sabre – long and sharp enough to settle any sort of an argument – as well as an impressive looking pistol in a leather holster with an ammo belt with about a hundred bullets – and each of those bullets were growling – like a row of tiny brass-covered pit bulls.

"The growling bullets were Sam's idea," Coyote said. "Ghosts can do that sort of thing. The bullets don't shoot any straighter, you understand, but their growling can sure intimidate the heck out of any possible perpetrator."

Bigfoot just stood there, like he didn't even actually notice the tall man's bullet-growling approach.

"Did you boys forget how to do your job again?" the tall man asked, in a voice that probably could have registered on the Richter scale.

"Sam," Coyote said, stepping forward to greet the tall man. "It's like this."

Only before Coyote could say another word the tall man just stepped directly through him.

Coyote fell on the dirt and lay there shaking like he had climbed out of a refrigerator sunk onto the bottom of the Arctic Ocean.

I went to him and helped him back up to his feet.

"I hate it when he does that to me," Coyote said. "But that's something else that ghosts do nearly any chance that they get. He likes walking through people and giving them the shiver-shakes just the same way as the big guy likes to yell."

"You shouldn't really ought to stand in the way of the law," the tall man said over his shoulder, towards Coyote and me. "I've warned you plenty about standing in my way before."

"We've got a situation here, Sam." Bigfoot said. "We thought maybe you could help."

"There is no help for the likes of you," Sam replied.

"So he is supposed to be some kind of a ghost?" I whispered to Coyote.

"That's the ghost of Sam Steele," Coyote told me – as if I should have known that in the first place.

"If we leave him out in the rain will he rust up?" I asked – trying to sound a little more braver than I actually felt. "What with him being made of steel, and all."

Only nobody laughed at my "steel" pun – which wasn't all that funny in the first place - but I had a bad habit of making jokes every time that I got scared.

And if I got any more scared than I was right now I ought to think about making myself a lifelong career as a stand-up comedian.

"Sam is a story, just the same as us," Bigfoot explained. "The real Sam Steele was one of Canada's very first Mounties. He died way back in 1919 – almost a hundred years ago - after fighting with the Fenians, chasing Louis Riel during the Red River Rebellion, meeting in a sit-down wiki-up with the great Sitting Bull himself, single-handedly taming the Klondike and fighting a half a thousand Boers over in Boerland."

He was a story?

I tried very hard to swallow that.

It went down like a mouth full of fresh frozen octopus.

"Is that true?" I asked the tall man.

The tall man snorted in amusement.

"Most of it is true," he told me. "Not all of it, you understand, but the gist of it is mostly true – if you squint at it awful fearsome and hold your mouth just a little to the left."

"In certain parts of Canada," Coyote went on. "Sam's actual stories have grown to a near mythic stature – thanks to a handful of novels and a half a thousand newspaper articles and a movie or two and campfire tales and once even a CBC minute vignette commercial."

"They even named a mountain after Old Sam," Bigfoot said. "That's more than I can say about me."

"They got it wrong, though," the ghost of Sam Steele said. "Mount Steele is actually only Canada's FIFTH tallest mountain. The way I see it they ought to have saved the tallest peak for hanging the name of Steele upon."

"It only stands to reason," Bigfoot said wryly. "I expect it must have been nothing more than an oversight."

"That's one more way that a story can be born into this world," Coyote further elaborated. "After Sam's adventures had been told and retold and inevitably exaggerated upon, his legend had slowly taken form and his ghost rose up and eventually assumed control of the Spiritual Operations Branch – otherwise known as the SOB's. The three of us – me, Coyote and Winnie are part of their tactical branch – otherwise known as the Creep Squad."

"Sometimes known as the Canadian Creep Squad," Bigfoot added. "Not that there is actually an American Creep Squad."

"We're unique," Coyote said.

"Actually, it is only known as the Creep Squad by those small-minded folk who don't have any sort of a sense of ceremonious propriety," the ghost of Sam Steele replied.

"Which makes Sam my boss of the Creep Squad," Bigfoot said. "Which makes him the fellow that I sometimes have to listen to."

"That and a generous helping of intelligence coupled with manly good looks," the ghost of Sam Steele added. "As far as I can tell I am a natural-born leader – but enough about me. Why don't you tell me what the problem is?"

Coyote and Bigfoot told the ghost of Sam Steele everything that had happened.

They told him about the Spirit Bear and Raven and the mauling of my stepdad Warren.

The whole thing didn't sound any more plausible than it had while I was actually experiencing the entire sequence of events.

"What do you think, Prophet?" the ghost of Sam Steele asked the travel home. "Do you think that you can actually track the Raven?"

"Might be I can," the Prophet replied. "But I would need a whiff of his scent."

"Be a good boy and go get that for me – now would you Fuzzy?" Sam Steele asked Bigfoot.

I did my best not to chuckle over his use of Fuzzy.

Bigfoot stepped back outside of the giant pink Winnebago.

"Are you coming?" he asked the Coyote.

"I wouldn't miss it for the world," Coyote said. "But somebody had better stay close to the kid, just to be safe."

By "kid" he meant me.

I didn't like the sound of them using that word "kid" but there really didn't seem to be much I could do to correct it.

"Allow me," the ghost of Sam Steele said.

Before I could say anything like "No" or "Let me think about this." or "I want an adult." or "I think I hear my mother calling me" the ghost of Sam Steele picked me up by the scruff of my Batman backpack and unceremoniously carried me on outside the motor home quicker than you say "Quick, to the Batmobile, Robin."

"Remain calm, boy. You have just been duly apprehended," Sam Steele said. "Kindly restrain yourself – or I will have to do it for you."

He was being awfully polite for a jerk, I thought.

"I liked you a whole lot better when you were just being a Mountie ghost walking through stray coyotes," I said. "Do you think maybe now you might want to put me down?"

"What makes you think I will do anything of that sort?" Sam Steele asked.

"Well, for starters, I might cry a whole lot and that might hurt your ears," I said. "Not to mention how hard it is to get tear stains and snot streaks from off of red serge."

Sam Steele chuckled softly to himself and then he dropped me down in the dirt, almost directly beside the dead bear.

Which was right about the moment when that dead bear opened his eyes and stood back up on his feet and growled.

Mostly at me.

Chapter Seven – There is more than one way to skin a dead bear

So I just lay there looking up at what looked to me to be a totally-zombified back-from-the-dead ursoid Spirit Bear – standing directly in front of me so close to my nose that I could smell the deep-crusted toe jam percolating nastily between the claws of his bottom feet.

"Hey bear - don't you know when you're supposed to be dead?" Bigfoot warned. "Am I really going to have to knock you back down again?"

The bear didn't look nearly as lively as it had before. It had turned a distinct shade of blue – like that funky old blue Gorgonzola cheese that my Great Uncle Wilbert used to like crammed in between slices of burnt pumpernickel toast. The bear's eyes had gone all flat and dark, like a sheet of slate after it had been rained on for about a dozen years – and then maybe dipped in black paint.

The bear shambled over towards us.

"There is just no way that he should be up and walking," Coyote said. "Not after a hit like that from a fully-grown Bigfoot."

Bigfoot growled a little.

"It might be that you're losing your edge, Old Fuzzy," Sam Steele taunted, drawing his pistol. "Not being able to knock down a Spirit Bear. They say that's the first thing to go in a Bigfoot – is his punch. Do you want me to maybe shoot him a few times and maybe soften him up a little bit before you try again?"

"Yes!" I frantically shouted. "Will somebody please just freaking shoot this big ugly zombie bear before he eats me?"

It lumbered a little closer.

"He isn't a Zombie Bear," Coyote corrected. "He's actually a Spirit Bear. They're a whole lot more trouble than Zombie Bears. Killing Zombie Bears is easy. You just shoot him in the head or use a flamethrower on him or else read the poetry of Stephen Vincent Benet."

Sam Steele took careful aim with his cannon-sized pistol.

"Zombie or Spirit Bear," Sam Steele said. "I can nail him colder than a fresh frozen flounder if you like."

Bigfoot just stood there and laughed.

"You've been firing blanks for way too many years, old man," Bigfoot said. "You put that big old pistol away before your hurt yourself with it."

"Well the way you hit him sure didn't put him under," Sam Steele pointed out. "I don't imagine me shooting him could do any worse of a job."

I could not imagine that I was going to die in the middle of a debate between a Sasquatch and the ghost of a retired Mountie.

"Well, I just guess I'll have to hit him again until it sticks," Bigfoot said.

That bear was getting closer.

"Somebody please hit him then," I begged. "Somebody PLEASE just freaking hit him right now."

If somebody didn't hit somebody soon my next home was going to be inside that Spirit Bear's stomach – and I wasn't looking forward to that whole experience. I wondered if the Prophet was intending to cocoon me up just the same as Warren – or else maybe they were just figuring on wrapping the two of us up together in the very same cocoon.

"You just don't know what's good for you, now do you – you dirty old Spirit Bear?" Bigfoot asked. "Trying to scare a little boy like that is apt to get me irritated."

That did it.

"Trying?" I shouted. "What makes you think he is TRYING to scare me? He is freaking well succeeded in terrifying the living bejeepers out of me."

By now everybody was laughing.

Bigfoot, Coyote, Prophet – even the Ghost of Sam Steele seemed to think the idea of that big Spirit Bear eating me was funnier than a polka-dot barrel full of drunken howler monkeys. As for me - I was still working on getting used to hearing an eight foot tall dust bunny with teeth talk out loud the way that Bigfoot was doing – much less listening to him laugh at me.

The Spirit Bear just growled a low wet slobberish sort of growl.

Or it might have been a chuckle.

"Oh go ahead," I told the Spirit Bear. "I give up. I surrender. Just eat me and put me out of misery why don't you?"

Bigfoot ignored my attempted surrender; bending over and picking up a boulder about the size of a good sized stand-up television set.

"Do you want to play catch, bear?" Bigfoot asked. "Is that what you want?"

The Spirit Bear kept walking up towards us.

I could hear great black wings beating darkly with every step that the Spirit Bear took towards me.

Bigfoot just stood there and waited with that television set sized boulder poised over his big shaggy head.

The Spirit Bear took two more steps closer.

And then Bigfoot dropped that big television set sized boulder so that it bounced and landed on the Spirit Bear's two big sized feet.

The Spirit Bear opened its mouth and roared in sudden unexpected pain.

"I saw a waiter in a movie do this once with a tablecloth and a dining room table full of fancy high tea fancy china," Bigfoot said as he reached out his right hand and crammed it fist-first directly inside of the Spirit Bear's wide open mouth. He caught hold of something inside that mouth that might have been a jawbone or maybe a set of tonsils or maybe even the inside-end of the bear's unwashed pooper-hole. Then Bigfoot reached out his left hand and caught the Spirit Bear by the throat and then he yanked that big old Spirit Bear inside-out.

"Smooth move," the ghost of Sam Steele complimented. "Did you practice that maneuver much or was it just dumb beginner's luck?"

"I think it was a little bit of both," Coyote said. "With the emphasis on dumb."

"You just sit there and take notes, kid," the ghost of Sam Steele said to me. "You can tell your grandchildren about what you saw today – assuming you live that long."

Which wasn't exactly that comforting of a phrase to hear.

"I always wanted to try it for myself," Bigfoot went on – like he was talking about a particular card trick he had just recently mastered. "I'm glad I finally got the chance to try it."

I couldn't believe what I was seeing. It was like something that you would see in a Saturday morning cartoon – only this time it was happening for real.

What came out of that Spirit Bear's mouth was a little like a tangle of blood and guts and smoke. It blew away in Bigfoot's big hairy hand like the smoke from a half a hundred birthday candles, Thick and cloudy and then gone all at once.

Bigfoot picked up what was left of the spirit bear's skin.

He gave the spirit bear skin a big old sniff.

"Do you even smell anything?" Coyote asked. "Or are you just blowing your nose out of pure blue-eyed spite?"

Bigfoot shook his head.

"We're going to need a better nose than I've got," Bigfoot said.

Coyote sniffed the dead spirit bear skin as well.

"I got nothing," Coyote said.

"I know that," Bigfoot said, jerking a thumb in my direction. "In fact the kid knows that. You got nothing, you'll never have nothing – heck you were most likely BORN with nothing and you've been slipping into the negative zeroes ever since – even the dead bear knows that much. There's no real reason to go bragging about it."

Coyote stuck his tongue out at Bigfoot – who pointedly ignored him.

"How about you, Winnie?" Bigfoot asked, holding the skin of the Spirit Bear directly beneath the Prophet's bumper. "It was your idea to hunt for scent in the first place."

Only the Prophet couldn't find anything either.

Bigfoot turned to look at me.

"Do you want to sniff it too?" he asked, holding what was left of the spirit bear's pelt in my general direction. "No sense you feeling left out."

I just looked away.

I didn't even want to see that Spirit Bear pelt, much less smell it.

"I didn't think so," Bigfoot said, stepping right over me and walking back towards the alder Winnebago. "Bring the kid, would you?"

"I can walk on my own," I said, before Coyote could pick me up again.

"See that you don't trip over your own two feet," Bigfoot said before walking back into the Prophet. "Or I'll drop a rock on them too."

"I don't think he likes me," I confided to the Coyote.

"Bigfoot doesn't much care for anyone that he meets," Coyote allowed. "Being the last of the Sasquatch will make a fellow more than just a little stand-offish."

Coyote and I stepped back into the Winnebago.

"Strap your seatbelts on," Bigfoot ordered, sitting down at the steering wheel. "I already know that Winnie can't tell us anything either."

"I heard you say that," the Prophet complained.

"So what?" Bigfoot asked.

"Friends don't insult other friends," the Prophet said.

"Who said that I was your friend, Winnie?" Bigfoot asked. "I'm just the guy sitting behind the steering wheel."

The Prophet said nothing.

I'm not sure – but I'm pretty sure that giant pink mystical travel home was about to have himself a long and proper sulk.

"What about Sam?" I asked.

"He can find his own way home," Bigfoot said.

And sure enough – when I looked back at the forest the Ghost of Sam Steele had already vanished into the shadowy darkness.

"Ghosts do that," Bigfoot said. "It is a part of their union rules."

Ghosts have unions?

"So are we going to visit the Old Man?" Coyote asked.

"I thought we just did?" I said, still thinking about the ghost of Sam Steele.

"Not that Old Man. We're talking about Nanna Bijou," Coyote said to me – as if I had to be seventeen kinds of foolish to not know just who or what they were talking about. "So are we going to call on the Old Man?"

Bigfoot smiled a great big how-stupid-a-question-was-that sort of grin in reply to Coyote's question.

"So who else are we going to call?" Bigfoot asked. "The freaking Ghostbusters?"

I shrugged.

"Let's roll," Coyote said.

And that's just exactly what we did.

We rolled – right onto the High Highway.

Chapter Eight – The Sleeping Giant of Thunder Bay

THE PROPHET'S ENGINES rumbled and growled about as loudly as a slow rolling avalanche of megaphone-yodeling angry buffalo as we began to move forward. I could hear The Prophet's big pink shiny wings flapping like the boom of giant cotton candy thunder.

"How in the world are we going to get through all of the trees?" I asked. "This motor home isn't exactly built for agility."

"The Prophet doesn't travel through the trees or over the trees or even under the trees," Coyote said. "He kind of moves between the spaces that lie between the spaces between the sky and forever. We call it riding the High Highway. It's a little more like flying above the sky – only we're faster and harder to catch."

Coyote was leaning against the Warren-cocoon.

I thought about the way that Warren always used to stand up whenever my Mom walked into the room – like he thought he was some sort of a Duke or an Earl. I thought how about how I had always thought that behavior was a little gorky – but now I wasn't really sure just what I thought about the whole situation.

I wasn't even all that sure just how I was supposed to feel about him leaning against what used to be – what still was, I guess – my stepfather Warren.

It felt a little too casual – almost disrespectful.

But I had to admit that the Warren-cocoon also looked pretty comfortable.

And – truth to tell I was still just a little uncertain about how I really felt about how I felt about Warren. All this time I had grown very comfortable loathing and despising my stepdad and here all of a sudden I was feeling caring and protective and I wasn't sure if this was some kind of a weird mood-swing that would change just as soon as the wind changed its direction or if this was something that had grown up in my spirit that I was just going to have to hurry up and get used to.

"Do you want to run that by me again?" I asked. "Using a few less syllables and a little more slow?"

"Listen, it's just basic science," Coyote said. "Everything in the whole world is made up out of atoms, right? But the Prophet, he's figured out a way to move through the spaces between the atoms of existence – only it's a little finer than that. It is a little like dodging raindrops. You dodge enough raindrops and you'll never get wet."

"So is that what you guys do?" I asked. "You drive around all day dodging raindrops and killing random Spirit Bears?"

"That's just some of what we do," Coyote said. "We work for the SOB – the Spiritual Operations Branch. It's a semi-official para-mystical anonymous working division of the Royal Canadian Mounted Police. Like Bigfoot said, some people call us the Canadian Creep Squad."

I had to stop and shake my head at that.

"So you're some kind of a Royal Mounted Creep squad?"

"Well, we're a lot more than that," Coyote explained. "The RCMP is just who we happen to work for, is all. And they don't even like to talk about us all that much. Truthfully, if you asked them, we don't even exist."

"So what are you then?" I asked. "Mutants? Aliens? Super heroes?"

Coyote thought about that.

"I guess what we really are when it comes right down to it," Coyote finally told me "Is nothing more than stories."

I shook my head at that explanation, too.

"Bigfoot over there," Coyote said. "He's the last of the Sasquatch. People have been telling stories about him ever since the days of Mesopotamia when storytellers would talk of Gilgamesh and Enkidu and the hairy wild men."

It was funny. If I had heard those names at home they would have meant nothing more than a bowlful of barely-cooked syllables. Yet hearing them here, inside of the Prophet's belly, I had the same kind of feeling as if I were listening to someone speaking of hamburger and pizza and chocolate milkshakes. I knew and I remembered the taste of those words. I felt those words splashing upon my back like great drops of a totally undodgable warm summer rain.

Somewhere deep in some part of me I knew the names that Coyote was saying – like they were distant relatives that I had overheard Mom or Dad or even Warren talking about one time or another. I couldn't put a face on any of those names but I kind of felt like I ought to know them just the same.

"Sure," I said. "I've actually got that part of it figured out. But how does that make you what you are?"

"Well," Coyote said. "Every time that you tell a story it is a little like dropping a small pebble into a bucket full of rainwater. There is a splash and then there are ripples and then there's an echo and that water fills up just a little bit deeper. You tell that story often enough and hard enough and long enough and the water splashes out of the bucket it sort of takes on a sort of life of its very own. "

That explanation didn't make much sense to me and I told him so.

"I can't really explain how it actually happens," Coyote went on. "It's not like we storied folk come equipped with any sort of a user's manual. But so long as storytellers tell our stories than we continue to live on in the borderlands that haze and drift between those lines that almost separate the cold steel truth of reality and the warm pure campfire smoke of our collective imagination."

"That still doesn't make much sense to me at all," I said, shifting around so that I could lean on the Warren-cocoon too.

Coyote chewed over my question some before speaking again.

"Just think about it this way," he said. "Let's say some kid tells some other kid in your school a story about how that kid that always sits in the back of the class that wears one of those big funky old hoodies – well, let's say that kid says that the other kid is really a Martian and he's wearing that big baggy funky old hoodie to hide the fact that he's really got a third arm duct taped to his ribcage, underneath the overly-large bagginess of the hoodie."

"That's stupid," I said.

"Sure it is," Coyote said. "Martians don't have three arms. They've got six, anyone knows that. But if that kid tells another kid who tells another kid then thirty years from now somebody's great-great-grandkid is going to be telling everyone about this three-armed Martian that went to school in the town that he grew up in and everyone will begin to wonder if maybe there couldn't actually be some truth to the rumor. I mean, it's thirty years ago, right? Nearly anything could have happened thirty years ago."

I nodded slowly.

That story almost made sense if you squinted.

"Well, you tell that story for a hundred years and somewhere in some far-off parallel dimension that three-armed hoodie-wearing Martian kid is going to be born. That's the power of good honest storytelling," Coyote explained. "If you tell a story long enough and strong enough and before you know it's going grow its own legs and learn how to walk, talk and breathe."

It still sounded about as stupid as stupid could get – but how could I argue with it? I mean, here I was driving around in a magic Winnebago with a Bigfoot and a Coyote.

Not to mention the Ghost of Sam Steele.

"Okay," I said. "I think I've got that. But why does Bigfoot have to drive? If The Prophet knows where he's going why does he need someone to drive him around?"

"It's how the magic works," Coyote said. "I'm not really sure why – but someone has to be behind the wheel before The Prophet can ride the High Highway."

"That doesn't make any kind of sense either," I said.

Coyote shrugged.

"Who says rules have to make sense?"

Which made even less sense.

"Why else would there be rules then?" I asked.

"Look," Coyote said. "Think about all of those Walt Disney cartoons. Why couldn't Pluto talk if Mickey and Minnie and Goofy and Donald could talk?"

I couldn't answer that question.

I wasn't sure if it was because the question was just plain stupid – or if Coyote was making some kind of crazy brilliant sense.

"Why didn't anyone ever rub the djinni lamp and use their first three wishes to wish for three more lamps?" Coyote went on.

I couldn't answer that question either.

"Rules don't ALWAYS have to make a sense," Coyote concluded.

I guess he had a point.

Either that or I was just stupid.

"So where are we going to?" I asked.

"We're going to talk to talk to Nannabhozo – the Sleeping Giant of Thunder Bay."

Hold it.

"You mean a giant – like fee fie fo fum?"

"That's another story and don't you dare be bringing Jack into it. He's way more trouble than we need right now." Coyote replied. "No sir, this is a story of the Anishinaabe – the people that you white men used to call the Ojibwa. Nannabhozo or Nanna Bijou – depending on what side of the Great Lakes you are standing on - is kind of special to me. He's a Trickster God – which makes him one of my spirit brothers. "

"Wait a minute," I said. "So you are some kind of a giant too?"

"I can be if I want to," Coyote said.

"And you are also some kind of a trickster god?"

Coyote looked away for a minute.

"I'm not in that line of work anymore," was all he'd tell me.

He said it quietly and then he looked away in that kind of way that some folks have of not talking directly to you – and I had the feeling that I wasn't about to hear the whole story.

"But we were talking about a Nanna Bijou story," Coyote went on. "At the time of this story he had settled from all of his Trickster days. He had grown old and had decided that he wanted to raise himself a family. So he decided that he was going to take care of the people who lived on the Isle Royale – just outside of the city of Thunder Bay."

"So how did he do that?"

"Well, he taught them how to fish for themselves and how to hunt for themselves and how to take care of their own selves," Coyote explained. "Just the way a real father takes care of his children."

I thought about all of the times that I had wished and imagined that my real Dad had found the time to teach me about hunting and fishing and his tattoos. I know that Warren did his best trying to teach me how to throw and catch a football and how to do math and how to run so that I did not look like an arthritic penguin – but that wasn't the same as my real Dad showing me things.

Was it?

Still, I could really understand just exactly what Coyote was trying to tell me.

"Another time Nanna Bijou fought Paul Bunyan for forty days and forty nights before finally beating him to death with a freshly caught giant Red Lake walleye," Coyote went on. "Although the way that Bunyan tells it he always says that he just let old Nanna Bijou win, on account of that whole fight was starting to look way too much like work to him."

I thought about that.

"Wait a minute," I said. "So how does Paul Bunyan tell that story if he got beat to death with a fish?"

"Death isn't what you think it is for us storied ones," Coyote said. "We only die when the very last story is gone and forgotten – which, if we're lucky, might mean forever."

"So you know Paul Bunyan?" I asked.

"Sure, doesn't everybody?" Coyote replied.

"I thought he was just a tall tale," I said.

"Ha," Coyote laughed. "Bunyan is tall all over – not just in his tail."

A part of me was surprised to hear that Coyote actually knew Paul Bunyan – but I was way too busy trying to figure out why every now and then the memory of Warren – my gorky stepdad – standing in front of that fully-grown Spirit Bear with his arm stuck out like a crossing guard crept into my imagination and just confused the living heck out of my sense of what is and what isn't supposed to be.

"After a while the Ojibwa of the Isle Royale began to refer to Nanna Bijou as the Spirit of the Deep Sea Water – which was kind of funny because Nanna Bijou had started out life as a sort of a Rabbit God – and he was always a little bit afraid of deep cold water – on account of so many of his kind had been dropped into deep old stew pots."

Coyote licked his lips loudly – and I think he was actually thinking about rabbit stew – which probably wasn't all that polite of a thing to be thinking about seeing as we were just getting set to visit ourselves an actual giant sleeping Rabbit God.

"The trouble all got started when Nanna Bijou discovered himself his very own silver mine and he showed it to his people and his people got to build themselves a bit of a reputation for having some of the finest silverwork in all of the country," Coyote said. "Only it got worse when the white man decided that he was going to find out where all that silver came from."

"You do realize that I'm white, too," I pointed out. "Don't you?"

"I won't hold that against you," Coyote replied. "We all have our various short comings. Besides, I have it on good authority that the Great Spirit is actually color blind."

By now I was hunched over and leaning forward – totally caught up in Coyote's story. It might have been because the whole thing was laid out in such a weird and twisty come-here-and-go-away sort of style that I had to lean in and focus just to follow it – but the fact was I was ACTUALLY kind of interested in hearing him tell it just the way he was telling it – mixed up weird or not.

"So what happened then?" I asked. "Did they try to shoot him?"

"Well those white men they tried all kinds of tricks. They had tried bribing the Ojibwa and they had tried torturing the Ojibwa but no matter they did they couldn't find themselves an Ojibwa who could tell them just where that silver mine actually was."

Then he paused and he sort of smiled and he looked off to his left like he was seeing the whole thing playing out before his eyes.

"But what happened next?" I almost screamed. "Something HAD to happen, didn't it?"

"Of course something happened. Sooner or later something always happens," Coyote said. "That's just the nature of life. One day an Ojibwa hunter took his pelts in to the white man's fort to trade for whatever he could get – but he made the mistake of bringing a few chunks of silver from the mine. So the white man traded whiskey with the Ojibwa and they got him to drink it and they drank with him only they were drinking every time he thought they were drinking whiskey and before you knew it they had talked him into taking a canoe and paddling them out to that silver mine."

It was strange sitting there and listening to Coyote's story. I had my i-pod wires still hanging around my neck and I could have easily have plugged in and tuned out but I was totally caught up in his words. And while Coyote was talking I'll swear that a little campfire seemed to grow up between us and cast its light and flicker and dance all about us.

"Well he took those greedy white men right out to the mine and they could not believe their eyes," Coyote went on. "There was more silver in that mine than they had ever dreamed of – but while they laughing and dancing and gathering up just as much silver as they could cram and stuff and jam into their backpacks and pockets they did not pay attention to a great dark cloud that rose up above them."

"It started to rain?" I asked.

"No, it did not start to rain. It was the shadow of Old Nanna Bijou and he laid down right on top of that silver mine, trapping those white men down there with all of that silver and then he cried himself to sleep on account of finding out how his people had gone and let him down and then all of those big old buckets of tears they crystalized about his body and hardened up and turned him into stone."

"He cried himself into stone?" I said. "That doesn't make any kind of sense at all."

"The tears of gods and mean are a strange and mysterious kind of magic," Coyote said. "You don't know what you will make out of sorrow until sorrow falls upon you."

"So what happened after that?"

"If you hush long enough I will tell it to you."

So I hushed.

I just HAD to know what came next.

"Well sir, they found that Ojibwa trader lying in his canoe scared clear out of his mind and they never found a sign of those white men and for all I know they are still down there in the darkness of that mine, counting their silver. And that mountain still lays there on that island, just off of Thunder Bay in that big old gulp that men call Lake Superior – and you can see it laying out there in the water if you look right out that front window."

So I looked out that Winnebago front window and I could see The Sleeping Giant of Thunder Bay lying there, stretched out in all of his wonder and his glory.

"How'd we get here?" I asked. "The last time I looked we were in Cape Breton."

"We got here by magic," Coyote said. "Weren't you paying attention?"

"Magic isn't real," I pointed out.

"Neither is Bigfoot – or screaming sacred sea monkeys, for that matter," Coyote replied. "The fact is – magic is real if you believe in it – or even if you don't."

"If you two are done with all of your talking," Bigfoot said. "We're going to come in for a landing. It's time to go and talk to a mountain."

I held on tight and waited for things to get worse.

The way things were going I didn't figure I had all that long to wait.

Chapter Nine – The Breath of the Great Lakes Dragons

WE CAME IN from a long way up.

"I like this part of it best of all," Bigfoot said. "I like seeing the way that everything down there that is so big looking so darned small from way up here."

The way I figured it nearly EVERYTHING must look small to a guy the size of Bigfoot – but I did not argue the point with him. I could see clouds around us through the windows of the mystic Winnebago. I didn't like to think about just how high we were but the land down below us looked like something that might have been built for a model railroad set.

It was a first for me. I had been on airplanes many times before – but this was the very first time that I had been this high up in a mystic pink Winnebago motor home.

"Do you see all of that deep green down there below us?" Bigfoot asked me. "That's the Sleeping Giant Provincial Park down there."

We moved in a little closer.

"Shouldn't we be careful?" I asked. "There are an awful lot of airports in Ontario. What if we wander into somebody's flight path?"

"They won't see us," Bigfoot said. "We don't even show up on their radar. Remember that rain cloud that you saw back in Cape Breton – the one that old Coyote jumped off of? That was Winnie, in one of his many spirit forms. Anyone sees us at all – well all they see is a rain cloud and a bit of dust blowing in the wind or just a soft pink mist."

That particular bit of knowledge still didn't comfort me all that much.

"Not seeing us wouldn't stop an airplane from crashing into us, now would it?"

Bigfoot just snorted, like he thought that was saying was one of the ten most stupidest of statements of last three centuries.

"We haven't hit anyone in a long, long time," Bigfoot said. "Why don't you stop worrying so much?"

That still didn't help me feel any better.

"The island looks a little bit like a raven, lying on its side, now doesn't it?" Bigfoot asked. "Can you see it?"

I looked down at what he was looking at. I could see how somebody might have thought it looked like a big old crow lying on its side.

Coyote wasn't so sure about that, though.

"If you ask me it doesn't look a thing a thing like a raven," Coyote said. "I'm pretty sure that the island looks just exactly like a coyote."

I took another look.

I really WANTED to agree with Coyote but I was still seeing a raven.

"I can see the beak," I said. "I'm afraid it doesn't look much like a coyote at all."

"That that little bit of island is called Thunder Cape," Bigfoot said. "And that is right where we are aiming to land on. Now you just keep your mouth open and your tongue still or else your ears will surely pop."

I looked out through the Winnebago window and I could indeed see a long peninsula that did sort of look like a crow's beak.

"There's a thick fog down there," I said. "It looks like it might be growing right out of the rocks."

"They call that fog the Dragon's Breath," Bigfoot told me. "Or at least that's what I have heard tell."

"You know - you know an awful lot of names for an awful lot of things," I said. "Can you tell me what my middle name really is?"

I was trying to be a wise guy, seeing if I could stump Bigfoot but I might as well have been trying to convince the wind to change direction.

"How about Irritating?" Bigfoot asked. "I think that sounds like a pretty good middle name for you."

Actually, my middle name was Aloysius – and I'm not going to tell you how to pronounce that. I had been named after an uncle who I really wish had been named something cool like Brock or Rip or even Knuckles.

"Is there any real dragons down there?" I asked.

Hey, if there was a giant down there – then why not a dragon?

"The Dragon's Breath is just a natural phenomenon," Bigfoot explained. "It is caused by the cold water hitting the sun-warmed rocks of the beach."

I wasn't all that convinced of what he was telling me.

"If you say so," I replied. "It still looks awfully dragon-like to me."

I studied the ground closely. We were still a long way off but if there were any dragons hiding down there in the rocks I didn't want to be caught unaware. It might sound stupid to you – but I had just seen a Bigfoot, a spirit bear, the ghost of a Mountie, a giant raven, a flying coyote and now we were going to visit a sleeping giant.

The possibility of me actually meeting an entire horde full of Winnebago-eating Great Lake Dragons didn't seem all that far-fetched to me at all.

"I still say it doesn't look a thing like a raven," Coyote repeated. "It looks more like the muzzle of a great noble animal – like maybe a coyote."

I guess he wasn't going to let that go until we agreed with him – but Bigfoot only snorted in disdain.

"If you squint, maybe," I allowed, trying to make him feel better. "I could probably see a coyote."

Bigfoot just snorted again.

I was just about to offer him a handkerchief to blow his nose with - when I spotted the very first dragon.

The first dragon came up out of the cold waters of Lake Superior. It was a long necked thing with the head of a lynx and two great horns on top of his head. He kind of moved like a tentacle on the end of an octopus – so long as that tentacle had a head on it the size of a freaking Volkswagen. The other noticeable feature was a long row of sharp-looking spikes right up the monster's long old backbone.

"DRAGON!" I shouted.

Actually, there were three of them.

Three giant freaking dragons.

"I wasn't expecting them," Coyote said. "Were you?"

"Me neither," I said.

"Relax, kid," Bigfoot said. "Those aren't dragons. Not really, anyway. They are more like a KIND of dragon."

"Does that mean they are only going to KIND of eat us alive?" I asked. "If they are I'd like the opportunity for a few last words and maybe even a grilled cheese sandwich and a bag full of potato chips."

The first not-really-any-kind-of-dragon reached its neck up out of the water and caught hold of the rear left tire on our flying Winnebago.

A part of me wondered just how often a fellow like me could be expected to think a sentence out loud as ridiculous as that last one sounded.

"They're big trouble, just the same," Coyote said. "They are what the local people used to call the Michi Peshu. They live in the storms and the high water of the deepest parts of Lake Superior. The Ashinabe used to calm them down with gifts of tobacco and prayer."

"Do you happen to have any tobacco?" I asked Bigfoot.

"I've never smoked," Bigfoot said. "It stunts your growth."

Then he looked at Coyote.

"Here," he said. "You take the wheel."

Which is the very last thing that Bigfoot said, right before he opened up the side door of our flying Winnebago – leaving Coyote to jump into the driver's seat – like he knew exactly what Bigfoot was going to do.

And maybe he did.

"I've got to fly," Bigfoot said.

Right before he jumped.

Out of the side door of the Flying Winnebago.

Forget about Superman - you WILL believe that a Bigfoot can fly.

Chapter Ten – Faster Than A Turkish Half and a Half Hitch Reef Knot

I DON'T REALLY think that there is any real way of getting used to the sight of an eight foot tall hairy anthropoid in midflight - especially when he is jumping out of the door of a giant pink flying Winnebago motor home.

"GEE-RON-AH-HOO-HAW!" Bigfoot yelled as

he hurtled downwards.

"Do you think he might hurt himself?" I asked the Coyote, who was busy keeping the Winnebago in the air.

"That depends on what he lands on."

"Shouldn't you be trying to help him?" I said.

"What, and spoil all of his fun?" Coyote replied. "Take it from me, kid. Bigfoot actually likes this part of his work. You watch and see – he's awfully good at it."

I supposed that Coyote was right. After all, Bigfoot was only jumping from about twenty feet up and that lake water looked pretty deep.

He ought to land with a fine and comfortable splash.

Only he didn't land in the water.

The second Mishi Peshu not-quite-dragon snapped at Bigfoot who sort of twisted in mid-fall and caught hold of the long row of spikes that were step-laddered up the monster's long backbone. Then Bigfoot hand-over-handed up the monster's backbone, swinging from spike to spike like some kind of a great ape trapeze artist.

The third Mishi Peshu not-quite-dragon tried to take a bite out of the neck-clambering Bigfoot that was clambering his brother's backbone.

I suppose it could have been his sister's backbone. I mean, there was really know of telling whether each of these Mishi Peshu's were actually a boy or girl.

"Come here, ugly." Bigfoot called out, catching hold of the third Mishi Peshu's lower jawbone with one big hairy fist and sort of twisting the beast's head sideways with pure brute force.

Meanwhile the first Mishi Peshu kept a firm mouth-hold of The Prophet's rear left tire. I guess it figured that there was no way on earth that a tiny little Bigfoot was going to be that much trouble to a pair of full-grown Mishi Peshu.

That just shows you what he knew.

Or she.

"Shouldn't you at least try and do something about that dragon that is hanging onto our Winnebago's tire?" I suggested to Coyote. "I mean, how puncture proof ARE we?"

"The Prophet is perfectly capable of taking care of himself," Coyote said. "Just you watch and wait and see."

By now I was beginning to get the idea that Coyote wasn't all that fond of any form of face-to-face confrontation. In fact, if I hadn't seen him with my own eyes falling out of the sky onto that spirit bear back in Cape Breton – even though he missed – I would have begun to suspect him of outright cowardice.

But he was right about the Prophet.

When the first Mishi Peshu not-quite-dragon bit down on the Prophet's rear left tire there was a sound sort of a like a low rumble of summer thunder crossed with a loud cheek-flapping bean fart. The Mishi Peshu's head swelled up like a balloon that had one one too many puffs of breath forced in.

Then that first Mishi Peshu hissed like a wet cat and slithered backwards into the deep cold waters of Lake Superior.

The air around the flying Winnebago grew green and funky.

"See," Coyote said, holding his nose tightly with his front paw. "I told you that the Prophet could handle it himself."

I wasn't sure if I could handle it. That green tire funk smelled worse than a road-killed cabbage-fed skunk in the middle of a hot summer day.

Bigfoot didn't look to be doing so well either.

The third Mishi Peshu – the one that Bigfoot had been hanging onto by the jawbone had shifted his mouth and bit down on Bigfoot's fist. Meanwhile the other Mishi Peshu had caught hold of Bigfoot's other fist and the two of those lake monsters looked to be trying their level best to make a wishbone out of Bigfoot.

"You've got to do something!" I said to Coyote.

Coyote sort of shrugged and lifted his hind leg towards the open Winnebago door and then he did what dogs do best and let a little warm smelly yellow rain fall down upon the ears of the two lynx-headed monsters.

"Most cats just hate it when you do that to them," Coyote said. "Even the big cats hate to get wet."

"Yeah," I said. "But that's still pretty gross."

"You told me to do something," Coyote said, with a shrug. "So I did it."

"That wasn't quite what I had in mind." I replied.

Still, Coyote's contribution did actually manage to distract the second Mishi Peshu for about a half of a half a second. Bigfoot made the most of the smelly diversion, hauling the second Mishi Peshu's neck around the third by pure brute force.

"Let's see if I remember how this works now," Bigfoot roared. "The little rabbit comes out of the hole and then he runs down under the log and then he jumps up over the log and then he heads back into its hole and the holes close up – right over left and left over right makes you a knot that's tidy and tight."

It was a little like watching the world's biggest hairiest Boy Scout tying himself a great-great-great-granny knot.

"Yes sir, I love to see a craftsman at work," Coyote said.

"How does that look to you two?" Bigfoot asked us.

I took a look. Bigfoot had tied the two Mishi Peshu's long necks into a regular granny knot – faster than you could say Baden Powell Boy Scout.

"I think the proper question is more accurately WHAT is that?" I said.

"That there is a proper Turkish half and a half hitch reef knot," Bigfoot happily announced, as we landed beside him on the shores of the Thunder Cape. "I didn't really want to go and hurt them. They are an endangered species, after all. This way I figure that it will take them at least a week and a half of full-grown tomorrows to untangle themselves. By then they will be hungry and they will head for the deep water and get out of our hair."

Which sounded reasonable.

As for me, I just wrinkled my nose in a great show of pure freaking disgust.

Knots or not, nothing reeks harder than a soggy wet and partially peed-on Bigfoot.

<u>Chapter Eleven – Talking to a Mountain</u>

BIGFOOT DROVE THE giant pink mystical Winnebago straight down onto the farthest end of Thunder Cape.

I was a little surprised that he didn't make more of a mess of it. The pink mystical Winnebago was about the size of Nebraska and I figured there ought to be leaving some sort of a trail of knocked-down trees behind. Maybe even a few turned-over tire ruts and at least a bump or two – but it looked as if the trees just sort of leaned out of the way of the Winnebago and the rocks and the bumps smoothed out before us.

"So where is this Giant hiding anyways?" I asked. "I kind of think that he would stand out a little bit, wouldn't he?"

"We just landed on him," Bigfoot replied. "You've really got to learn how to open up your eyes and LOOK."

So I took a long look around.

All I could see was a high cliff shooting up, with trees and rocks and maybe a few birds drifting overhead – most likely wishing that they had flown to somewhere interesting.

"Big freaking deal," I said. "It looks a whole lot like Cape Breton to me – or any other part of Canada that has rocks and trees instead of a city in it.I don't know about you but I think we haven't really gone anywhere at all."

"That's the problem with you city boys," Bigfoot said. "You were born with a pair of eyes that you just don't know how to use. You look around and all you see are rock and trees and the same blah-blah-blah, when the actual truth is that every single part of Canada looks and smells and sounds different."

"It's all in the way that you squint," Coyote said – which made about as much sense as a pickle flavored ice cream sundae –

but I forgot all about how foolish their words were to me when Nanna Bijou - the Sleeping Giant suddenly sat up.

Have you ever seen anyone buried in the sand on a beach?

You know how some people like to be covered in sand with just their head and their nose sticking up out of the dirt. That particular pastime never did make all that much sense to me – or maybe I just wasn't squinting properly at it – but seeing the Sleeping Giant sit up from out of the rocks and the trees of Thunder Cape looked almost exactly like watching someone sit up on a beach and shake the sand from out of their ears.

"Hey Old Man," Bigfoot said.

"Hey Little Fuzzy," the Sleeping Giant said. "How have you been doing?"

I had to giggle a bit at that.

"Little Fuzzy?" I asked Bigfoot.

Bigfoot looked down at me a little like the very same exact way that I would look down at an ant crawling across my boot laces.

"Maybe I might be little to him," Bigfoot said. "but not half as much as you look little, standing next to me."

"Are you trying to tell me I'm short?"

"What I'm trying to say," Bigfoot replied. "Is that whenever you are standing next to me you look as if you are standing barefoot in a very deep hole."

Well, I might have argued that particular mathematical formula with him but I couldn't see all of that much of a future in debating arithmetic with an eight foot tall Sasquatch Bigfoot who could talk to a mountain.

"Hey Nanny Bozo Long Socks," Bigfoot said, deliberately getting Nanna Bijou's name wrong just to bug him a bit. "How the heck are you doing?"

"I'm not doing too bad at all, Mister Short and Fuzzy and Funky-Smelling," Nanna Bijou replied. "How are things going for you?"

"Shorty, eh?" Bigfoot replied. "Do you know what the Russian Cossacks say about dwarves fighting giants?"

"How would I know?" Nanna Bijou asked. "I've never learned to speak Russian."

"Well, let me tell it to you," Bigfoot said. "According to the Russian Cossacks a dwarf will beat a giant every time. All that the dwarf has to do is to reach straight up as high as he can reach and yank down hard twice."

I had to laugh out loud at that – being a keen appreciator of the grosser forms of pelvic humour.

"Shh," Coyote hushed me gently. "It is very bad manners to laugh in front of a mountain."

I took his word for that and stopped laughing.

"I have come to ask you a favor," Bigfoot said to Nanna Bijou.

"I didn't think you'd come all this way to talk about the weather," Nanna Bijou replied. "So what exactly all are you looking to know?"

"I brought you this to look at," Bigfoot said, holding the skin of the spirit bear up towards Nanna Bijou. "What do you think of it?"

Nanna Bijou reached down one hand.

As big as Bigfoot was, seeing him next to Nanna Bijou was a little like watching a ten year old playing with an action figure. I just had the feeling that old Nanna Bijou could have just as easily have snatched up all three of us and thrown us clear across the country.

Still – looking at that great mountain giant didn't give me too much of a sense of fear whatsoever. He looked calm, almost peaceful, like somebody's favorite grandfather – only not quite so funny smelling. His eyes were like deep calm pools and I swear to you that I could see trout jumping in them and I was likewise sure that if I had managed to get close enough I would have seen frogs kick-swimming through those deep calm eye pools of old Nanna Bijou.

His face was cracked and creased like he was about a billion years old – but he still had the ghost-memory of a smile creased and cracked about the corners of his mouth. I was pretty sure that Old Nanna Bijou still thought of the world as being a very cool and neat and wonderful place – kind of the very same way that a two year old kid will look at a playground.

He took that funky old spirit bearskin from Bigfoot's extended hand like it was nothing more than a scrap of tissue for blowing his nose on. He held his palm up to his face carefully, like the palm of it was full of salt and vinegar potato chips, and then he waved his other great hand over his upraised palm, wafting the scent of the spirit bearskin up to his mighty great nostrils.

We need a better nose, Bigfoot had said.

Looking up from my perspective I had to admit that I had never seen a set of nostrils as large as Old Nanna Bijou's were. They were like weird great teepees full of mystery and boogers the size of small downhill boulders. I had the feeling as if there might have been great colonies of bright green booger-bats hiding up in the caves of those huge and mighty nostrils – and a weird freaky part of me wondered what they looked like inside.

If ANYBODY could tell us where the Spirit Bear had come from – this guy could.

"Do you recognize the scent?" Bigfoot asked.

A thundercloud passed over the features of Nanna Bijou. Just for an instant I could see some of that strong dark power that

Old Nanna Bijou – the Spirit of the Deep Sea Water – must have still possessed.

"It is not a good smell, that is for sure," Nanna Bijou said. "It is a very bad smell and it belongs to this one's brother."

Nanna Bijou pointed down at Coyote who sort of looked like he was trying to hide in the shadow of a nearby tree. I wasn't certain if Coyote was feeling embarrassed or afraid – or maybe even a little of both.

"I was pretty certain that the Spirit Bear had been called by Raven," Bigfoot said. "I just wanted to be good and sure, is all."

"Do you really plan to hunt down Raven?" Nanna Bijou asked.

"Now what do you think we are planning to do?" Bigfoot replied with a slow sly grin – which told me that Bigfoot didn't quite trust Nanna Bijou – not any farther than he could throw the big old mountain giant.

"I think you might better off finding yourselves a deep dark cave to hide down in for maybe about the next hundred years or so," Nanna Bijou said. "Raven won't be all that easy to take down."

"First I've got to find him," Bigfoot said. "I'll let the taking-down part figure itself out once we get there."

Nanna Bijou thought about that.

"You will need a good tracker," Nanna Bijou said.

"I can track," Coyote replied. "Coyotes are actually natural born hunters."

"No offence – but I know that you couldn't find the wrong end of your tail if you used both of your paws and your teeth," Nanna Bijou said to Coyote. "No, I think you folks really ought to look up the Ku Sidhee."

"Old Shuck?" Bigfoot asked. "The Death Dog?"

"That is the one," Nanna Bijou said. "You will need to go back to Cape Breton – back to where you came from."

"You've been watching us?" Bigfoot asked. "You must have been if you know where we have come from."

"I sleep with one eye open," Nanna Bijou said. "But who is this with you? I have been watching him but do not recognize his story."

"My name is Adam Rooker," I said. "I am very pleased to meet you Mister Mountain, sir."

All right – so you tell me just exactly how you would go about addressing a mountain?

Old Nanna Bijou, he seemed to like that though. He chuckled a little, turning loose a couple of small scale avalanches.

"Sir, is it?"

"Yes sir," I said. "I mean, your mountainship sir."

Bigfoot put his hand over his mouth trying unsuccessfully to hold back his laughter and Coyote was rolled over and giggling out loud but Old Nanna Bijou just looked down at me and smiled.

"This one has been raised properly," Nanna Bijou said. "You two lug-nuts could learn a thing or two about respect from this little Adam story."

Now Bigfoot started laughing as well.

I ignored their shared hilarity.

"Can you keep care of him while we hunt for Raven?" Bigfoot asked.

"I don't need anybody to take care of me," I argued. "Let alone a mountain."

Nanna Bijou laughed at that, too.

"This little Adam story has been marked by the Raven," Nanna Bijou said. "You know what that means now don't you?"

Bigfoot nodded.

"It means that I am stuck with him," Bigfoot said. "Until we fix things right."

"Hey," I argued. "Don't I get any kind of a say in this?"

"He has got a point," Coyote said. "It is his life that we are talking about after all."

At that point I was getting awfully tired of standing there and being talked about like I had about as much to say about my own fate as the last pork chop on a fat man's plate.

"So what's it like being a mountain?" I asked, butting into the conversation just as hard as I could manage.

"It isn't so bad, little Adam story," Nanna Bijou said. "But the days can get awfully long. I grow tired of listening to the birds and the wind. There's only so many times you can listen to some red-bellied robin telling you how big of a worm he just caught."

I thought about that.

I guess I could understand what he was telling me. It wasn't all that hard to imagine just how boring it could be just sitting there on the end of an island at the edge of a lake and listening to a whole lot of nothing worth listening to.

And then I did something completely unexpected.

"Here," I said, handing him my i-pod and headphones. "They're a little small – but maybe you ought to try wearing these."

Old Nanna Bijou reached down and he carefully plucked the i-pod and headphones from my hand. It felt a little like feeding a shelled peanut to a fully grown elephant – but as he picked up the i-pod the wires seemed to grow and stretch as long as telephone pole wires – which I guess was magic. The headphones enlarged – I could see them swelling up bigger and bigger the closer he got them to his big old mountain-god ears.

Then he popped them right over his ears and I almost at seeing just how big he was smiling at the sound of the Squealing Sacred Sea Monkeys screeching out Misunderstood #23.

"Hey," Nanna Bijou said. "This is even better than that Johnny Cash tone-deaf hoedown hoohaw that Little Fuzzy listens to all of the time."

Seeing Bigfoot scowl the way he did at that last comment made the whole thing worthwhile.

"Go ahead and keep them," I said. "They look good on you."

Nanna Bijou smiled at that.

I guess he was feeling pretty happy with the gift I had given him.

"Nice one, kid," the Coyote said. "You're a natural."

"Beginner's luck," Bigfoot growled softly.

Old Nanna Bijou looked down at me earnestly.

"You have done me a great kindness," Nanna Bijou said. "And I would like to return the favor. What gift can I give to you in return?"

"He's offering you a wish, kid," Coyote explained. "It's like a favor – only bigger."

"Why?" I asked, suddenly a little nervous.

"You paid him due homage," Coyote said. "Which means that you gave him a gift. That's a sign of politeness to the old people. Which means that he has to give you a gift back – only it needs to be even bigger than your gift was."

All right.

A freaking wish.

That had be cooler than an iceberg in a deep freeze.

Now I have got to admit that the very first thing I thought of wishing for was a pot full of shiny gold.

I mean, here was this mythical magic mountain giant standing in front of me like a genie out of a lamp and asking me to make a wish.

So that's the first thing ANYONE thinks of – isn't it?

A million dollars.

A pot of gold.

All of the freaking money in the whole freaking world.

But then I thought about what I'd do with that money and I thought of how easy money was to spend and I thought about just how fast money vanishes once you started spending it and then I thought to myself why not wish for what you REALLY want.

So then I said it.

I said what I really wanted to wish for.

"If I tell you what I wish for that means you have to give it to me, right?" I asked.

Nanna Bijou nodded.

"Think carefully, kid," Bigfoot warned. "You might not like getting whatever you try wishing for."

Says you, was what I thought.

I was DONE listening to Bigfoot.

"No matter what I say," I went on. "You have to give it to me."

Nanna Bijou nodded.

"Careful," Coyote warned nervously. "Be very careful."

But I already knew what I was going to say before I even said it.

"I want to see my Dad," I said. "I want to see my real Dad – before he found that baby carriage and went and died."

And then Nanna Bijou nodded for the third and final time.

And then all at once I was gone.

I had the distinct feeling I was going to feel deeply sorry for what I had wished for.

Chapter Twelve – Shaking Hands With the Raven

WHEN IT HAPPENED, it happened fast.

It was like a cloud had somehow got in the way of the sun. Everything blurred just a little and I worried for a moment that maybe I was going to faint from an overexposure to one too many outbursts of unbelievable stupidity. Maybe I was having some sort of a seizure and maybe I was going to die right here on the shores of Cape Thunder.

Maybe I'd even get to see Dad.

My real Dad.

Maybe this was how Old Nanna Bijou was going to grant my wish. Maybe he had just struck me dead with magic and I was going to finally get to see my real Dad.

Oddly enough the possibility of me actually being dead wasn't terrifying me half as much as it probably ought to have.

Only I wasn't dying.

Things were just getting darker, was all.

I had seen a YouTube video of a squid shooting ink once. It looked a little bit like what was happening to me right now. It was as if the entire world was growing darker but just in the spot around me as if I had somehow stepped into a state of permanent shadow.

I glanced back over my shoulder. Bigfoot and Coyote were standing right where I had left them, still looking away from me and up at that walking mountain, Old Nanna Bijou. I could see the sun was shining on the two of them but it was as if I were looking at the sunlight through a half a dozen pairs of dirt-stained dark glasses.

Only Bigfoot and Coyote weren't moving at all. They were both standing perfectly still as if they were nothing but a cartoon on television that somebody had paused. I could see a bird flying over Coyote's left shoulder only the bird wasn't moving, either. It was hung there like it had been thumb tacked to the sky.

"I was wondering just how long it would take you to get here," said a voice about as dark as the shadow in the bottom of a two hundred foot well-hole. "Usually what I leave my mark on comes back to me a whole lot quicker than this."

The voice I heard was a voice that sounded about as dark as the darkest of dark bitter chocolate bar, if chocolate could sing - only it did not sound not half as sweet as that.

I looked up to see just who was talking to me.

I think he would have probably stepped dramatically out of the shadows except I think he was made completely out of shadow. He was tall and lean and wore a magician's top hat that smoked like the old tin chimney that sat on the roof of my real Dad's summer cabin. As the shadow man stepped towards me he kind of shimmered as if he were made out of shadow, smoke and road tar. It looked to me as if every black Crayola crayon and last-forever Sharpee marker had been smeared and smudged across his soul.

Now what?

Where had Old Nanna Bijou sent me?

"Pleased to meet you," the shadow man said – reaching out and shaking my hand.

I just stood there and I said nothing – repressing the sudden urge to count my fingers to make certain they were all intact after he had shaken them.

"Can't you speak?" the shadow man asked. "Did the crow steal your tongue?"

Don't say anything, I thought to myself.

Don't you dare answer this freaking weird shadow man.

Don't you dare say a single freaking word.

"Crows will do that, if you are not careful," the shadow man said. "They will steal your tongue right out by the roots."

Not a word.

Whatever happens please don't say anything to me. I'm just a kid on a summer vacation. I'm in Cape Breton and you are not Darth Vader and this is NOT the twilight zone. I am just bonding with my dorky stepdad, Warren.

No more of this freaky weirdness, please.

"Do you believe in monsters, Teller-boy?" the shadow man asked me.

He reached out to me just the same way a shadow will reach out as the day grows longer. I felt a passing coolness and a heat, like I was standing in the shade of a hot and breezeless August afternoon. I smelled attic dust and wind-blown feathers and the kind of crispy ash that sticks to freshly-burned marshmallows.

I suppose I should have said something.

I shouldn't have been as scared as I was.

After all, I had lived through my Dad being blown up by a baby carriage. A little thing like a man made out of shadow and ash should not have terrified me like it was doing.

"Do you believe in monsters, Teller-boy?" the shadow man repeated.

I opened my mouth.

My lips were dry and stuck together. My swallow had disappeared somewhere on the other side of the Gobi Desert –

probably riding on a camel train of cotton balls and talcum powder and those weird little packets of silica gel that you find at the bottom of your vitamin jar.

I had forgotten how to make words follow one another. I had forgotten just how to string thought together into anything close to making sense.

But I had to say something.

"No," I said. "I don't believe in monsters and I don't believe in the Tooth Fairy and I don't believe in the Easter Bunny, either."

Where was Warren when I really needed him?

Where was Bigfoot?

Where was Nanna Bijou?

"You are awfully young to be acting so cynical," the shadow man said. "When did you learn to not believe in a story told true?"

"Monsters aren't real," I said, scornfully. "They're mythological."

"Mythological?" the shadow man said. "That is a pretty large multi-syllable-mouthful of a word for a little bitty kid like you."

Kid?

"I'm seventeen years old," I said. "That makes me a teenager, not a kid. Do you want to hear me recite my A-B-C's?"

"Only if you can say them backwards."

So I turned around backwards, looking away from him, as I began to recite.

"A, B, C, D, E..."

Which I thought was pretty funny – but when I said it out loud the words I was speaking didn't come out as A-B-C-D-E.

It came out as B.C.W.F.C.O.T.F.O.H.E.

I felt those word-letters spilling out of my mouth like I had chewed into a bowl of apple sauce and come up with a mouth full of cast iron apple seeds.

"And a case of freaking nails," the shadow man finished up. "Isn't that what you were trying to spell, Teller-boy? Isn't that what really killed your Dad? Of course I mean your real Dad, not your step-dad Warren – isn't that what really and truly killed him?"

I opened up my mouth.

I closed it.

So far as I could tell no words fell out in between.

"Look at me, Teller-boy," the shadow-man said.

I don't do anything for people who end a sentence aimed my way with the word "boy", but it was as if he had hold of my puppet strings. I turned like my feet were built on a set of well-oiled steel swivels.

"My name isn't Teller," I said. "That's my step-dad's last name. I keep telling you people that my real last name is Rooker."

"What do you know about rooks, boy?"

I didn't have an answer for that.

"Look at me," the shadow man repeated, dropping each word at my feet like a single fallen drum beat.

And then the shadow man began to change.

He began to spread as if his shoulders were somehow slowly separating. I saw long dark wing-shadows stretching out above us. I felt like one of those old movie cowboys – like I had been crawling across the desert dying of thirst and looked down to see the buzzard shadows circling about my dying body.

The shadow man was Raven.

The shadow man was the same giant magic bird that had stolen the spirit bear. He was the same giant magic bird that had stolen a piece of Warren's spirit.

I didn't get it.

Why had Nanna Bijou sent me to the guy I was trying to run from?

Did he want me to die?

And then I began to change too.

I hate it when that happens.

Nothing sucks worse than change.

Chapter Thirteen – In Which I Grow Wings

I FELT THE change happen slowly, like I was drawing the entire transformation inside of myself in a long slow drawn-out breath. I felt something soft and fluttery being dragged and pulled and tugged from out of my bones. I felt veins stiffening and sharp shooting pain shouting out as if someone were sticking giant white hot darning needles into my skin and then yanking them back out fast.

I felt as if my blood was made out of something like the ocean and the sky above the ocean was on fire and everything inside of me had just begun to boil.

I squeezed my eyes closed and for just a moment I saw nothing but a long swallow of midnight black.

I heard a giant crow laughing over me – with a harsh caw.

I wondered just what was so funny.

And then I opened my eyes.

There was nothing but clear blue and patches of white cloud. I could see my feet hanging beneath me only they had stretched out into hard yellow sticks.

No, not sticks.

Talons.

Bird feet.

I looked down at myself and then I realized that somehow I had been magically turned into a giant crow.

"You just feel that you are a giant, is all," I heard the shadow man talking above me. "You are not really a giant at all. You have seen a giant before, haven't you, Teller-boy?"

I knew that he was talking about Old Nanna Bijou and for about the hundredth time since the last five minutes I wondered why in the world did Nanna Bijou send me to see this freaking creep?

Were they friends or something?

Maybe partners?

What had Bigfoot got me into?

I looked up above me and all that I could see was a field of darkness. I felt a little like an aircraft trying to land on an aircraft carrier only I had got my directions turned around and the carrier was floating above me while I flew deep down in the water.

"You know," the shadow man cawed down at me. "For a fellow who only watches television and Youtube videos you have one heck of a peculiarly vivid imagination."

It was one heck of a little peculiar seeing a giant crow talking down at me in the middle of what had to be a nightmare in the middle of the day.

"I'm a raven," the bird corrected me. "You're a crow."

"What's the difference?" I cawed back.

I'm not really sure if I was cawing or talking or just thinking about cawing and talking but he seemed to understand me just fine.

"The old people will tell you that crows are nothing more than the shadows of every other bird in existence," the shadow raven told me.

And then he paused.

I knew he was waiting for me to ask.

So I did.

"So what's a raven?" I asked.

"A raven is the shadow of a crow grown giant-large beneath the promise of sunlight," the shadow raven explained. "A raven is everything that a crow has ever dreamed of ever becoming and then some."

He gave a sharp little flap of his wings in a style and a manner that could only be called smug.

"Isn't that somebody you know down there?" Raven asked, sort of half-pointing with the tip of his right wing.

I looked down and all of a sudden I could see what looked to be some sort of a village growing up below me.

What the freaking heck was going on?

That village hadn't been there before – or at least I hadn't noticed it down there.

And then, with one strong beat of his wings the shadow raven swooped down towards the dirt. Actually, I think he stepped onto an invisible elevator. He plummeted faster than I could even think about.

I knew I couldn't keep up with that kind of speed, so I just drifted down a little closer – thinking about autumn leaves and parachutes and those little tiny dust motes that always dance in sunbeams.

My wings worked – so far.

I looked downwards. I could see about a billion acres of gray sand stretching out below me. Further on I could see gray stone buildings cluttered about the sand like a small child's building blocks.

The scene looked both primitive and modern at the same time.

As I got a little closer I saw smoke drifting up.

There was a figure lying in the dirt.

"Come on slowpoke, the last one to make it to the lunch box was hatched from a rotten egg," the raven cawed out.

He swooped down past me like a jumbo jet in a drag race.

I flapped just as hard I could.

Wings or not, this flying business wasn't easy.

As I got a little closer I could see what I'd been looking at from my bird's eye view.

The figure was a soldier.

I could see the uniform.

It was my Dad.

My real Dad.

I knew that before I even got close enough to see.

"This is who you wanted to see, wasn't it Teller-boy?"

My dead Dad.

I flew down just a little bit closer, deathly afraid of what the Raven was going to show me next.

And yet I was still not able to turn away.

Chapter Fourteen – Food For The Crows

NO WAY - THIS could NOT be happening.

All I had done was to make a single stinking wish to a stupid mountain god.

The shadow raven circled around my Dad.

Closer.

Closer.

At least I think it was my Dad.

Remember, I hadn't seen him in about ten years, what with him being dead and all and mostly gone before that. And all I really had to go on were a few crappy photos in Mom's photo album and the stories that she told with each of the photos. I mean, you don't really remember things like how your Dad looks, if he dies when you are nothing but a teenager.

In fact – if it came down to it I don't believe that I had actually seen my real Dad for any real length of time since I was seven years old.

Now let me tell you, at seven years old you just don't really get much of a look at your Dad. All that you really see is just a big set of nostrils floating high above you. All that you really hear is a deep and lofty voice that floats every now and then and reminds you to "sit up straight" and "listen to what your Mother tells you".

That isn't all that much to go on.

"Come on, Teller-boy," the shadow raven cawed out. "There is enough fresh meat here for the two of us."

He landed on top of what was left of Dad's chest.

It wasn't all that pretty.

Especially after that baby carriage full of roofing nails had got done with it.

Dad's eyes opened.

He looked directly at me.

"You have to tell…" he began to say - and for the life of me I swore that I was hearing my Stepdad Warren's voice coming out of my dead real Dad's mouth.

It was getting AWFULLY confusing.

And then the shadow raven beaked down into the chili-con-carne of what used to be my Dad's chest and Dad's eyes closed just as quickly as they had opened and he stopped talking like his tongue had been torn out of his mouth.

The shadow raven beaked down and tore something long and wet from out of my Dad's exploded rib cage. I flew towards the shadow raven, trying to stop him before it was too late but it was WAY too late. The Raven smiled at me and I felt an invisible knife pressing against my brand new crow heart. I knew I had to be imagining the whole thing but I stopped breathing just the same.

I just hung there, hovering in mid-air, not even flapping my wings.

I don't know if crows can do that.

"So, do you believe in monsters?" the raven asked me, with a long string of Dad dripping down all thick and gooey from his beak. "Do you, Teller-boy?"

I gulped.

I nodded slowly.

The shadow raven smiled and it wasn't a nice kind of smile at all.

"Good," the shadow raven said. "It is important to learn something new, every day. And even if you are lying to me - even if you don't truly believe in monsters - you will, soon enough."

Then the shadow raven reached out to me, caught hold and pulled me in and through his own self. It felt as if I were diving through the middle of the memory of a rain puddle. I felt wet and dry and hot and cold all at once.

I felt it all rushing in at me, all at once.

I felt that exploding baby carriage going off beside my Dad. I felt what HE felt like when that case of roofing nails tore through what he used to call his body.

I remember screaming.

I remember that shadow-raven leaning down and whispering something into the wind tunnel of my left ear.

I remember hearing the words but not knowing what each of them meant.

Because I was still way too busy screaming.

And then all of a sudden I saw half of Bigfoot – the top half of him anyway – leaning out in thin mid-air. It was like he was standing on a stepladder, leaning out through a hole in the sky. All that I could see was his big fuzzy chest and his head and his long arms floating there above me as he reached down towards me.

"Come here, kid," Bigfoot said.

Then he grabbed me and pulled me clear out of my dream and into that hole in the sky that he was dangling out of.

Just in the nick of time.

Chapter Fifteen – Lies My Mother Did Not Mean To Tell Me

"IT'S AN AWFULLY darned good thing that I got to you when I did," Bigfoot said. "He almost had you r head turned clear around."

I think I might have nodded in reply.

The truth was I couldn't really be sure. I had come up out of that dream-walk screaming so loudly that it had taken Bigfoot and Coyote a full fifteen minutes of there-there, there-there, there-now-there to calm me back down to earth.

"So where did he send me?" I asked.

"Not too far," Bigfoot replied, looking away from me like he didn't really want to tell me the whole complete story of where Nanna Bijou had actually sent me to. "But you were very nearly far enough."

Of course, Bigfoot might just have been trying to spare himself the sight of me crying like I was three years old and somebody had just broken my favorite toy truck – only I didn't really care if anyone saw me cry.

I had just seen my Dad die.

I had felt the whole thing happen – just like I had died right there alongside of him.

I had felt it happen deep inside of me.

That was the worst part of it.

I couldn't stop thinking about all those stories and lies people had told me.

"It would have had to be quick," they always told me. "A blast like that and you'd be gone before you know it."

Everyone that I knew kept telling me that – every time I turned around at the funeral and for weeks afterwards.

It was like the only thing that people seemed to want to talk about.

I'd be sitting down at the supper table and I'd ask someone to pass me the potatoes and they'd look at me and say – "Well, at least it was quick."

Even my mother had stared me right in the eyes and told that lie to me.

"It had to be quick," she told me. "When your father died. It was over suddenly. He didn't feel any sort of pain."

I don't know who she had been trying to convince more with that single stupid lie – me or herself.

It wasn't quick.

It wasn't painless.

My Dad had felt every single stinking second of it.

Bigfoot kept on talking to me – the whole time I was lying there and shaking and crying and screaming. I could see his mouth moving but whatever he was saying the words kept bouncing off of my ears. I could still count, though – and as near as I could tell Bigfoot kept saying three single words – over and over and over.

Finally I heard what those three words were that he was saying.

"Are you okay?" Bigfoot asked – looking at me with a surprisingly deep concern spilling out of those great big sad Sasquatch eyes of his.

I almost wanted to laugh in his big hairy face.

Was I okay?

No.

I was NOT freaking okay. I don't even think I could spell okay if you shook out every single O and K and A and Y in the Scrabble game into my open right hand and pointed really hard at a dictionary.

In fact, I don't think I was EVER going to be okay again.

Okay?

"Yes," I finally said, just to shut him up. "I am okay."

Because that's what we do to people who we need to shut up – we tell them stories.

We tell them lies.

Just like the sort of lies that Mom had told me.

"You don't look all that okay to me," Coyote said. "In fact, you look about as un-okay as a person can get."

"I don't think un-okay is a word," Bigfoot pointed out.

I give up.

That's the thing about grown-ups – whether they're human or coyote or even a Sasquatch. No matter what you say to them it's NEVER the right thing. It's like God reached down and created us kids and taught us how to speak in Swahili and then he had reached down again and touched every adult on the planet and taught them how to listen in Ukrainian.

Maybe God was an adult too.

Or else maybe he was just another story.

"I'm okay," I repeated. "I'm okay, I'm okay, I am freaking okay!"

I was getting a little bit angry.

"I don't think you are saying what you think you are saying," Bigfoot said.

Which hurt my head a little just trying to listen to it.

"Okay – so I am GOING to be okay," I said – which was a little closer to the truth.

"Is there anything we can do to help you get there?" Coyote asked. "Before you get any more of your kid-snot smeared on my fur?"

I didn't have to think about that one bit.

"Yes," I said. "There's something HE can do."

And I pointed directly at Bigfoot when I said it.

"What's that?" Bigfoot asked.

"The one who did this to me?" I said. "That guy with the big black wings?"

Bigfoot nodded.

"I know who you mean," Bigfoot replied. "I know his name. We don't really need to say it out loud. I know just who you are talking about."

I looked Bigfoot right in the eye.

"I want to make him pay," I said. "I want to make him pay for what he did to me. "

Then I took a deep breath.

"I want you to make him pay until it hurts," I finished up.

Bigfoot just smiled.

"Just so you know," Bigfoot told me. "When it comes to payback you have definitely come to the right fellow."

I smiled right back at him.

I was ready for some honest-to-gods Raven payback.

You bet your Colonel Sanders feather-plucking chicken fryer.

Chapter Sixteen – Chasing Rabbits Only Makes Your Feet Sore

FASTER THAN YOU could say "go", Bigfoot had herded us back into the Winnebago – which by now was loudly snoring – and believe you me, you haven't heard ANYTHING until you have heard a giant pink mystical Winnebago snore out loud.

I'm not saying it was pretty.

We might have got there even sooner if Bigfoot hadn't stopped to take the time to frighten the blue jumping blazes out of a Thunder Bay Cub Scout troop. They had been setting up camp just beyond the shadow of Nanna Bijou. There was about twelve of those Cub Scouts - and as near as I could tell they were all busily watching their Cub Scout leader trying to start a fire with rubbing two sticks together, neither of them being a match.

At which point Bigfoot jumped out into the clearing and waved his hands in the air like he was being group-mugged by a horde of blackflies.

"WHUGBUGGABUGGABUGGEDY BOO!!!"

Bigfoot yelled out at the Cub Scout pack.

I am not exactly sure who jumped higher – the Cub Scout leader, the troop or me. We all hit a certain level of altitude and then fell back down into the dirt.

"So why did you have to do that for?" I asked afterward.

"I'm just keeping the dream alive," Bigfoot replied mysteriously. "The way I figure it they'll be telling stories about me all night long. A little bit of luck and somebody will tell a newspaper – which will bring in Bigfoot-watchers from all across the country. And then – when they aren't sitting out in the woods with their binoculars and their cameras and their motion detectors just trying to get a single Wikipedia-worthy photograph of me they will sit around their campfires and tell Bigfoot stories."

"So you mean the more that people tell your stories the longer you live?" I asked.

"To a point," Bigfoot explained. "There are rules that govern just how much a storied one such as me can expose my existence."

"So setting up a Facebook page would be out of the question?" I asked.

"You got it," Bigfoot said. "You give them a little peek – just enough to talk about – and then you make like magic and vanish."

"Show off," Coyote said.

"You're just mad that I saw them first," Bigfoot said. "You know as well as I do that the more people tell Bigfoot stories the more likely it is that I'll stick around."

"That's what you say," Coyote grumbled. "I think you're just blatantly displaying your innate exhibitionistic tendencies."

"You ought to be careful you don't sprain a lip," Bigfoot retorted. "Gargling with all of those multi-syllable words like you have been doing."

Which was right about when we reached the still-snoring Winnebago.

"Wake up, Winnie," Bigfoot growled, banging on the dashboard. "We're on a mission now and there's just no time at all for taking a nap."

"What about him?" I asked, pointing at the window at the mountain-god Nanna Bijou, who was lying happily stretched out listening to The Squealing Sacred Sea Monkeys on that i-pod I'd given him.

"What about him?" Bigfoot asked. "You want to give him some more of your music? The last time you did it you almost yourself killed."

"Or worse," Coyote added.

"He did this to me, too," I said. "If he hadn't sent me where he did I wouldn't have had to go through with what I did. The way I see it, he ought to pay too."

"I told you to be careful what you wish for," Bigfoot snarled. "Do you REALLY want to go and try talking smack to a living breathing mountain?"

"He gave you just exactly what you asked for," Coyote unhelpfully added. "As far as I could tell he wasn't really trying to hurt you."

"Heck," Bigfoot went on. "He gave you a story to tell. That's the most precious gift in the world, the way I see it."

I wasn't so sure about any of that.

"You two are afraid of him, aren't you?" I said. "That mountain – he's a whole lot bigger than you. I expect the two of you are scared totally stiff."

"Maybe old Coyote here might be scared of that big old trickster mountain god," Bigfoot said, jerking one big hairy thumb in Coyote's direction. "And I can definitely guarantee that Winnie the pink is scared out of his wits as well."

"I'm not afraid of anything," The Prophet argued – only he was whispering deep down in his wheel-wells when he said it.

"That's not really what I'd call fear," Coyote explained. "That's nothing more than simple common sense."

"What about you?" I asked. "Are you scared?"

Coyote looked at me like I was talking ten kinds of stupid.

"Of course he's scared," Coyote said. "He just won't admit it, is all."

"Wrong, wrong, wrong," Bigfoot said. "I am not scared of Nanna Bijou. I could take him down somehow – if I really felt I needed to."

"I know there's a big old hairy b-u-t hanging off of the end of that sentence somewhere," I pointed out. "Why don't you just go ahead and tell me why you aren't going to do anything about what that mountain god did to me?"

"Listen to the words that I'm telling you," Bigfoot said. "If you chase one rabbit, odds are you'll get yourself some supper. "

That made sense – assuming a fellow wanted to eat rabbit. I never had but I had heard some people say that it made a pretty good stew.

At least Elmer Fudd always seemed to think that Bugs Bunny would make pretty good eating in all of the cartoons I ever watched.

"But if you try and chase more than one rabbit at the same time and all you end up with is aching feet," Bigfoot went on. "And with feet as big as mine I don't need to add one more ache to my current personal hurting limit."

I still didn't get it.

I told Bigfoot so.

"I don't get it," I said – just in case YOU didn't get that.

"Right now, that mountain god is one too many rabbits for us to chase," Bigfoot patiently explained. "We might deal with him later – but right now we've got one thing and only one thing only that actually NEEDS to be dealt with."

"What's that?"

"We need to hunt ourselves a dog."

"A dog?" I asked. "What for?"

"We need a dog because I told you so," Bigfoot said.

There's nothing I hate more than being told "I told you so" by somebody bigger and older than me when all I'm really asking is "why".

I told him that too.

"You're not going to give up on this, are you?" Bigfoot asked.

"I want what I want," I said. "And I want it right now."

Meaning I wanted an answer.

"Close your mouth," Bigfoot told me. "Listen to what I am telling you. Stop talking right now and start thinking."

He bit each single word off slowly and carefully.

So I shut up.

I sat there and I thought quietly and just as soon as I did all that it came to me – why we were hunting a dog.

"We need a dog because we need to find a better nose to track Raven's scent," I said back, just as slowly.

"See," Bigfoot said. "I told you that you were going to learn something."

I sat back and I even grinned a little, feeling pretty pleased at me.

"All right," Bigfoot said. "Prophet, tune me in a little old school classic Hank Snow and see if you can pipe it into Old Nanna Bijou's headphones, would you?"

"Hank who?" I asked.

"Exactly," Bigfoot mysteriously replied. "Give him a little taste of Liverpool, Nova Scotia – now would you, Prophet?"

We took off just as Nanna Bijou sat up howling loudly in consternation as the Squealing Sacred Sea Monkey's off-key shrieking and skirling bagpipe fervor was replaced by whatever it was that Bigfoot had suggested Prophet pipe into his earphones.

We hit the High Highway and Bigfoot started singing and he didn't stop until we got back to Nova Scotia.

"That big eight-wheeler is a'rolling down the track, means your true-loving daddy ain't a-coming back - I'm moving on, I'll soon be gone," Bigfoot roared out. "You were flying too high for my little old sky so I'm moving on."

"Yeehaw," Coyote chimed in.

And then old Coyote started to yodel – and you haven't heard anything until you have heard a yodeling Coyote spirit.

I'm not saying it was pretty.

But oddly enough I sang right along with the three of them.

I didn't know the words – but it really didn't seem to matter.

I just hummed along with the story until I figured out how to get the whole thing right.

Chapter Seventeen – Following the Scent of Feathers

IT IS KIND of funny just how very much the passing of a little bit of time can change a person's outlook on life.

Five minutes following our departure from Thunder Cape I had begun to feel a whole lot different about listening to Bigfoot sing.

Bigfoot had slid on through Hank Snow's "Moving On", had sung straight through Boxcar Willie's "Wabash Cannonball" and we had snowplowed into Dave Dudley's "Six Days on the Road" – and the only reason that I knew that those were the names of each of the songs and the singers that had sung were because in between each horrifying song Bigfoot would pause and announce in a big old baritone broadcaster's voice – "And for my next song I'll sing…"

"Does he always sound this bad?" I asked Coyote – after I'd finally got tired of trying to sing along with him.

"Oh no," Coyote told me, grinning that ear-to-ear mile-wide Coyote grin. "Most of the time he' sounds a whole lot worse."

That was really hard to believe.

"It can GET worse than this?"

"I could always take a stab at harmonizing," Coyote allowed, with a sarcastic grin. "The Prophet blows a pretty mean car horn to and you've already heard my yodeling. If you knew how to play the guitar we could actually take this act on the road."

That sounded pretty bad to me.

"So why does he like to sing so much if he sounds so awful?"

Coyote shrugged.

"Because it's fun, I guess."

I thought about Warren's own terrible singing and the way that my Mom always laughed when he tried to sing.

The thought of my Mom laughing was even harder to think about than Warren's singing – so I tried to change the subject.

"Speaking of the road," I said. "Where exactly are we headed for? And how is this all supposed to help my stepdad Warren?"

I jerked my thumb at that weird pine needle and alder brush cocoon that used to be my step-dad. I still thought Warren was actually a bit of a dork, you understand, but I had become sort of invested in seeing that he gets back safe to Mom.

I'm not saying that I liked the guy any better than I had.

Don't you dare try and put words in my mouth.

"We're following a scent," Coyote explained. "Or at least The Prophet is – and Bigfoot is driving because that's how the magic works and we're just going along for the ride."

"So we are supposed to be following Raven, is that it?"

"Sort of," Coyote allowed. "Only he's too smart to leave himself a scent to follow."

That arithmetic didn't add up one bit at all.

"So if this Raven doesn't leave a scent, then what are we really following?"

"We're following the scent of the Spirit Bear that attacked your step-dad," Coyote said. "And, in a way we're kind of following the scent of your step-dad's spirit – which is what that Spirit Bear actually took from him."

"That only makes sense if you squint at it and blink hard," I said. "If Raven is as smart as you say he really is then why hasn't he done something to mask the scent of the Spirit Bear?"

Coyote looked away, like he wanted to change the subject.

Only I wouldn't let him get away with changing it.

"Did I use too many syllables for you?" I asked. "Would it help if I explained my question just a little more slowly?"

"Raven is smart," Coyote said. "That's a fact that is as true as the sky is blue – but he is something else besides that."

"What's that?"

"He is confident," Coyote said. "A little confidence can go a very LONG way."

Now I got it.

"You mean that he is over-confident," I said. "He thinks he's too good or too strong to worry about what we can do to him. Is that it?"

Coyote still looked like he wanted to talk about anything besides Raven.

"Is that it?" I repeated.

Finally he spoke.

"I didn't say he was over-confident," Coyote allowed. "The truth is he is every bit as powerful as he imagines himself to be. You have got to remember that it was Raven who stole the sun from the North Wind. It was Raven who ate the Father of the Whale People from the inside out. It was Raven who peeled the color from off of the Polar Bear's coat."

"So what color did polar bears used to be?" I asked.

"It depended on which way the wind was blowing," Coyote explained. "Sometimes green, sometimes red, sometimes blue when they were feeling sad."

Thinking about a green polar bear made me giggle just a little bit, which seemed awfully close to Coyote changing the subject so I decided that I didn't really want to know the answer to that particular question right now.

"So you're saying that this Raven character is pretty bad news," I said.

Coyote nodded.

"He's a trickster god – one of the oldest ones there are," Coyote said. "That means he usually thinks about four or five steps beyond our wildest dreams."

"Yeah, but you're a trickster god too, aren't you?"

Coyote shook his head and looked down at his feet.

"I'm not in that line of work anymore."

There was a story there. I knew there was but until I figured out how to read between the lines I'd have to settle for listening to just what he saw fit to tell me.

So I tried another approach.

"You seem to know an awful lot about this Raven," I pointed out. "Are you and he good friends?"

Coyote thought about that.

I let him think for as long as he needed

I wasn't in that much of a hurry.

"I wouldn't say we were exactly friends," Coyote finally decided. "But I know him about as closely as I know my own shadow."

I thought about that.

"And we can't take him, is that it?"

Coyote shrugged, just ever so slightly.

"But we are still following him," I went on.

Coyote nodded – barely moving a muscle in his neck.

"And when we catch up to him?" I asked.

He grinned.

"Well then we will see," Coyote said. "Now won't we?"

And then he smiled the kind of wild and crafty smile that sort of gave me the feeling that he might know just a little bit more than he was letting on.

Which was either a good thing – or not.

"Have I ever told you just how much I truly hate someone who answers a question with a question?" I asked.

"I suppose that I ought to do my best to remember that particular fact," Coyote replied. "Now shouldn't I?"

And then we were there.

Right back to where we started from.

Chapter Eighteen – A Billion Searches to the God of all Googles

I TOOK A long look around at where we had come to.

"This looks just exactly like Nova Scotia," I said. "In fact, it looks like the very same place that we started from. Are you really sure we are getting anywhere?"

"Give the kid a genuine cheap candy cigar," Bigfoot said. "Congratulations. You finally guessed something right."

"I guess there is a first time for everything," Coyote allowed. "There might even be a chance that hell will freeze over."

Ha-ha.

"So we went all the way from Cape Breton to Thunder Bay and then we came back again to the Cape Breton Highlands?" I said.

"Right again. Your sense of direction is nearly infallible," Bigfoot said. "Truly I stand in awe of your awesome-as-apple-sauce awesomeness."

I was getting used to his sarcasm in the same way as you might get used to the reek of an old rain-soaked sheepdog. That didn't mean that I liked it any better – that just meant that I was getting used to it which I guess goes to show that you could get used to anything.

"That's so funny I might even have to laugh at it for two or three times," I twice-as-sarcastically replied. "But maybe while you are in the mood for explaining things – do you could tell me who in their mind would EVER call this the highlands? None of it really looks one bit like a mountain range to me."

Coyote giggled.

"Kid," Bigfoot explained. "The Cape Breton Mountains are some of the oldest mountains on the Eastern coastline. They used to be a whole lot taller – until age and erosion and glaciers wore them down to what you see now – but if you look at them in a certain kind of manner you'll see the memory of the mountains they used to be."

"Are you trying to tell me that these are really the ghosts of mountains?" I asked.

"Actually," Bigfoot said. "They're more exactly the stories of mountains that used to be."

"Or better yet call them the memory of mountains," Coyote said.

"They still look like hills to me," I said.

"It all depends on you learning how to squint," Bigfoot said. "You listen closely enough and you can hear the glaciers talking."

I held up my hand up to my ear like I was listening.

"So what exactly are they saying?" I asked. "Because I can't hear a thing."

I half wanted to know and I was halfway trying to be a smartass about it. Teenagers can be perverse that way.

"I guess it depends on just who is listening," Bigfoot said. "To me they are telling a story about a time when there were nothing but Bigfeet as far as you could see."

"Was there ever such a time?" I asked.

"Who knows?" Bigfoot said, with a shrug. "It's a story. True doesn't have any place at all in this particular equation."

"So what are they telling me?" I asked.

I was a little less smartass about that second question.

The truth was, I really wanted to know.

"Well," Bigfoot began. "If you ask me these mountains would tell you the story of a boy name of Glooskap. One morning the people woke up and the rivers and the lakes had all run dry. It turns out that a giant bullfrog named Aglebemu had built himself a huge stone dam to keep all the water of the world for himself."

"Why did he want all of the water?" I asked.

"Water is part fish and that big old giant bullfrog monster wanted all the fish to his own self as well," Bigfoot explained. "But the boy named Glooskap went out and caught hold of the big old bullfrog and he swung him by his legs and cracked his back against the big old stone dam and the pieces of the dam flew in all directions and they soaked into the dirt of the earth and grew up into mountains and that is why the bullfrog is born with a hump on his back from the bruising that boy named Glooskap handed out to him way back at the day on the dam."

"So what is that supposed to mean?" I asked.

"It means that even a boy can make himself useful every now and then," Bigfoot said. "At least as far as killing frogs is concerned."

"Gee, thanks," I said.

"Anytime," Bigfoot replied.

I decided to give up on arguing over this particular issue.

"So what exactly are we looking for?" I asked. "Is this supposed to be the place where Raven is hiding out?"

Bigfoot growled loudly.

"So what did I say wrong?" I asked.

"Do me a favor and try and not say his name out loud outside of the walls of The Prophet," Coyote warned. "He could be listening."

"Who?" I asked, wanting to know just whose name I wasn't supposed to say out loud and WHO could be listening.

"Now this kid thinks he's an owl," Bigfoot grumbled. "Why don't you see if you can catch us a rabbit? Owls are supposed to be good at that."

"Well who do you think can hear us out here?" I complained. "There's nothing around here but a whole bunch of trees."

"And you don't think they're not listening?" Bigfoot asked.

"Trees don't have ears. Trees are plants. Nothing but bark and leaves on some and needles on the other. "

"Corn has ears, doesn't it?" Bigfoot said. "Why do you think that the most serious of gardeners all make it a point to sit and talk to their plants?"

That might have made sense if someone had hit me on the head with a rock about six or eight times before saying it to me.

"Because they are freaking weird, maybe?" I guessed.

"Look who is calling who weird," Bigfoot said. "You're the one who is having a conversation with an urban myth."

"Don't put on airs," Coyote said. "There's nothing urban about you."

This was getting nowhere fast.

I took a long deep breath, considering my next question as carefully as possible – barely resisting the urge to yell "Raven, raven, raven" at the top of my lungs – only the memory of me looking at that shadow-raven gnawing on my Dad was just enough to make me think better.

"Okay," I said. "So are we here in you-know-where looking for the scent of you-know-who, you-know-what?"

"Who?" Bigfoot asked.

"What?" Coyote asked – almost at the exact same time that Bigfoot spoke.

Even I had to laugh.

"What we're here for," Bigfoot explained. "Is we are looking for a better nose than I happen to be wearing beneath my eye holes."

"We are looking for a good hunting hound," Coyote went on. "What else did you think we came here for?"

What the freak?

"So we are looking for a dog?"

"We're looking for something like that," Bigfoot explained. "We're looking for a dog that could hunt out a single bead of sweat in a gymnasium full of sweated-up funky-pitted and newly-puberty-infested basketball players. We're looking for a dog that can hunt out a single second in an entire century full of long irritating minutes."

"Wouldn't a GPS be a whole lot quicker?" I asked. "Or maybe we could even try looking it up on Google – under D for dog."

"What we are looking for can't be found on any GPS," Bigfoot said. "What we are looking for won't even show up if you sacrificed about a billion searches to the God of All Google."

"You mean you-know-who?" I asked.

"I mean you-know-what," Bigfoot replied. "What we're looking for right now is a certain canine known as Old Shuck, the Devil's Dog."

Have you ever got an answer that didn't mean a thing to you when you finally got it?

This was one of those kinds of answers.

"So what exactly is a Shuck?" I asked. "And is an old one any better than a new one?"

"You tell him, Coyote." Bigfoot said. "You always tell it best."

"You mean I remember it best," Coyote corrected.

"Whatever," Bigfoot said.

I was getting tired of waiting.

"One of you had better tell the story to me, quick," I said. "Because I am running out of patience pretty darned fast."

Bigfoot snorted.

"Let me tell you a story," Coyote began.

Why did I know that he was going to say that?

I think these guys were MADE out of stories.

"Why don't you just tell me what you figure you need to tell me," I suggested. "And let's skip the whole story thing."

"I can't do that."

"Fine," I said.

"Fine," Bigfoot echoed, sulkily. "You'll sit and listen to HIS stories, but you won't sit and listen to MINE."

"What choice do I have?" I asked – but I already knew the answer.

Namely, none at all.

Chapter Nineteen – The Tale of Old Shuck – as Told by Coyote

"**THIS IS THE** way that the story was first told to me – way back when I was nothing but a pup," Coyote began. "Many, many, many long years ago."

"You mean way back when people lived in caves?" Bigfoot asked. "Back when they carried clubs and ate dinosaur burgers for breakfast?"

"People weren't actually around when the dinosaurs were," I pointed out. "My science teacher taught me that."

"What?" Bigfoot replied. "Haven't you ever watched the Flintstones?"

I gave it up as an argument that was already lost long before it ever got started.

"I'm not that old," Coyote angrily snapped.

"You're not that young, either," Bigfoot pointed out. "Besides, you only start the story that way in case you get any of the facts out of order – which you probably will - in which case you can always blame who ever told it to you first."

"Do you really want to try and tell this story all by yourself?" Coyote asked. "I'm not sure there aren't too many syllables in it for your vocabulary."

"Tell on," Bigfoot replied. "I'm not saying a single word."

"That'd be a first," Coyote retorted – but then he jumped right back into the flow of the story – before Bigfoot could squeeze one more wisecrack comment out of his mouth.

"It started with a young boy by the name of Little Billy," Coyote began. "A young boy named Billy who lived all by his lonesome out in the deepest darkest woods imaginable. "

I sat down on a rock.

I had the feeling this was going to be a long old story – because so far I hadn't actually heard any short ones - and I figured that I might as well do my best to make myself comfortable while I was at it.

"How come every question I ask you guys always has to lead to some dumb old story?" I asked. "It's beginning to become a bit of a habit."

"There is no such thing as a dumb story," Bigfoot said.

"Our whole existence depends upon stories being told," Coyote added. "So long as a story is told and told well we storied folk will continue to walk the earth."

"So tell it, then," I said. "Tell us all about that forest."

I was getting a little impatient.

"There were trees in that forest that were so old that you would have to spend three hundred years of straight night-and-day calculating just to count up how many rings run round the middle of their trunk," Coyote went on. "There were trees so old that their shadows had grown roots of their own and the roots had grown shadows. There were trees so old that their leaves had got all tangled up with the clouds and the moonbeams."

"Okay, okay," Bigfoot interrupted. "We got it. It was an old forest. Can you cut to the chase? I see my birthday coming up in about three months down the road and the way that you are winding up the wind you generate might blow out all of my candles before I even get around to thinking about baking myself a cake."

"You're interrupting me again," Coyote said.

"Well tell it to us in a hurry," Bigfoot said. "Life is too darned short for this sort of interminable monotony."

"That's what I'm doing," Coyote said. "I am telling it just as fast as I am able to."

"Well, tell it faster," Bigfoot said. "Before it gets too dark to follow the trail."

"How come he lived by himself?" I asked. "Didn't he have any parents?"

"Are you going to start interrupting now?" Coyote asked.

"I'm just asking is all," I said, with a shrug. "I still want to hear the story."

By then I did. It was funny, but every time that Bigfoot interrupted I wanted to hear it told all the more.

"Then I recommend listening a little more with your ears," Coyote said. "and exercising your mouth a whole lot less."

And then, before Bigfoot could add anything else, Coyote snapped at him.

"And you," Coyote snapped. "If you interrupt one more time the very next story I intend to tell is going to concern the manner in which you were discovered asleep on top of that used car lot roof with that giant latex blow-up King Kong mannequin."

Now that sounded like the kind of a story that I REALLY wanted to hear – but Bigfoot shut his mouth so fast that I swear I heard his jaw click shut.

So Coyote started his story again – completely uninterrupted.

"The boy didn't live COMPLETELY by himself," Coyote went on, answering my last question first. "He had parents – and I already told you that he had a dog."

I nodded hastily, not wanting to interrupt him any more than I had to.

The way I figured it, if either myself or Bigfoot interrupted him one more time it would be weeks and weeks and weeks before we ever heard the end of Coyote's story.

"Dogs are great companions – given that they aren't quite coyotes - and this dog was the boy's very best friend."

I nodded again.

Coyote seemed happy with that.

"The boy's name was Little Billy, on account of his Dad's name was Big William." Coyote went on. "The dog's name was Shukramarama – which was what Little Billy had named him – because at the time that he had named the dog, Little Billy was only about three years old and he had liked names that rhymed inside and the name Shukramarama had sounded cooler to him than an entire refrigerator full of fresh-frozen polar bear toes - but everyone else called the dog Old Shuck, because the name was shorter than Shukramarama. Little Billy used to live with his parents and his grandparents – but one summer that all changed."

I leaned in a little closer.

I hated to admit it – but this was beginning to get interesting.

"One hot summer night – when the moon was hanging in the sky like a fat rotting pumpkin – someone knocked on the family door."

"Who was it?" I asked.

"It was Old Man Death who had come knocking on the door," Coyote explained. "He had come for Little Billy's grandfather – whose name was Old William."

"Wait a minute," I said. "You mean there are THREE Billy's in this family?"

"Did their last name happen to be Goat-Gruff?" Bigfoot asked. "And did they go trip-trap, trip-trap, trip-trap over a long wooden troll bridge?"

"Shut up," Coyote replied.

"Was their mother's named Billy too?" Bigfoot asked.

"Shut up," Coyote repeated.

"Maybe they were a family of hillbillies," Bigfoot suggested.

Which was funny.

"Actually, there was Old William, Young William and Little Billy," Coyote explained.

"Where there's a Will, there's a way, I guess," Bigfoot said.

"Are you done shutting up?" Coyote asked. "Because I could still sit down and tell that latex blow-up King Kong story."

"I guess I'm done," Bigfoot said. "For now at least."

"And how about you?" Coyote asked before I could get my two cents in. "Are you going to let me finish this story?"

So I shut up again, for at least a half a breath or so.

"So Little Billy's grandfather Old William walked outside and walked away with Old Man Death," Coyote went on.

"Why'd the grandfather do that?" I asked.

"The grandfather was old and his bones had been aching for long past hurt and he figured that if he didn't walk away with Old Man Death that there might be trouble for the family."

This was a complicated story but I did my best to listen.

If it had something to do with getting Warren out of that pine cone cocoon and me back to somewhere close to the way that everything used to be – it was worth listening to.

"What happened then?" I asked.

"Well, three weeks later there was another knock on the door," Coyote said. "It was Old Man Death again – only this time he had come for Little Billy's grandmother, Wilhelmina."

Wilhelmina?

It figured.

"I thought you said her name wasn't Billy," Bigfoot interjected.

"It's Wilhelmina," Coyote said. "That isn't Billy, now is it?"

"If you say so."

"Well, she had been feeling pretty stiff and tired and old herself," Coyote went on. "So she went along with Old Man Death without making any kind of trouble. She missed her husband and she wanted to go off and be with him in the Kingdom of the Dead."

I leaned back against the Warren-cocoon.

It felt a little cooler – like the sun had been shining on it all day long but it was now time for the night to fall. That Warren-cocoon felt like it was growing colder and its breathing seemed to feel a little bit more labored and I had the feeling that Warren was dying.

I still wasn't sure just what that would feel like.

It had been hard enough losing one Dad, never mind losing a second.

"What's that feel like?" I asked. "Being so lonely that all you wanted to do was to walk off with Old Man Death? And what does the Kingdom of Death look like? Do they have any sort of computer games there?"

I wasn't sure if I was talking to Coyote or to Bigfoot or whether I was talking to whatever was left of Warren inside of that Warren-cocoon.

I might even have been talking to my real Dad.

"You won't know until you get there," Bigfoot answered. "And until then you just have to learn how to make do with just not knowing."

I wasn't so sure about that but I didn't see any point in arguing with him over it.

"Three weeks later there come another knock at the door."

"Was it Old Man Death?" I asked.

"It was," Coyote replied. "Well, Little Billy's father went to the door and told Old Man Death that he would have to go. You've caused enough trouble for this family, Little Billy's father said to Old Man Death. Why are you so set in picking on us? Then Old Man Death told Little Billy's father that sometimes it rains and sometimes and sunny and this was nothing more than Little Billy's family's turn to get rained on."

"Who did he come for?" I asked.

"Old Man Death had come for Little Billy's father – and try as he might, Little Billy's father had absolutely nothing to say in the matter. He hung onto the doorway and he hung onto the banister and he hung onto the porch swing but then finally he had nothing left to hang onto and so he got up and he walked on down the road with Old Man Death."

"What happened then?" I asked. "Did Old Man Death take Little Billy's mother?"

"He did not," Coyote said. "So why don't you stop trying to guess all of the fun out of this story?"

I thought about all of that family walking down the road with Old Man Death and I had to wonder just how much fun this story was REALLY supposed to be?

"Little Billy's mother cried for three straight weeks – from sun up to sundown until the pine floorboards of the house were soaked with her tears. And then on that night of the third week Little Billy's mother stood out on the porch under the moonlight and she sang a song that sounded a little like a coyote howling at the moon and the waves talking to the shoreline and the wind whispering through the autumn trees on the longest midnight of the year. She sang a song that was both beautiful and terrible and as lonely as an empty water bucket, rusted at the bottom and poked full of holes."

Closing my eyes and listening to Coyote's story I could almost hear that lonesome woman singing her song.

To the ears of my imagination that lonesome woman sounded more than just a little bit like my Mom.

"So what happened then?" I asked.

"Well Old Man Death, he heard the song and its music called to him just as surely as a southern dream calls to the bump on the front of a wild Canadian goose bill. Old Man Death just walked up to her porch and she told him that if he didn't take her there and then that she was going to keep on singing until the world filled up with tears and drowned."

"So what did he do?"

"What could he do? If the world all drowned he'd be out of the death business – on account of everybody getting suddenly drowned," Coyote said. "So he took her with him on down the road to the kingdom of death."

"Three weeks later a raging swamp fever hit that area and Little Billy took sick and he lay on his bed and he dreamed of wildfire and furnace coal. The heat roared up in him from out of bones and he sweated so much that his sweat soaked the floors clear of his mother's tears. Finally Old Man Death had nothing to do but to walk on up to Little Billy's house and take Little Billy down the road with him too."

WHAT???

"He doesn't die too?" I said. "That isn't fair!"

"Who said death was supposed to be fair?" Coyote asked. "Death is nothing more than a single card in a deck that we each have to turn over – one card at a time – until we reach that final card and the game is done."

I thought about my Dad lying out there in that desert – blown to ribbons by that baby carriage full of high explosives and roofing nails.

Sometimes it is sunny and sometimes it rains.

"So what happened next," I asked sullenly.

"Old Shuck had his own idea about where Little Billy was going to go," Coyote said. "When Old Man Death walked onto the porch Old Shuck was standing there and waiting for him. That dog growled a growl that would terrify a thunderstorm into sunshine. "

"Did he chase Death away?" I asked. "Did he save Little Billy?"

I was really getting worried.

"I didn't say that," Coyote said. "The truth of it was that Old Man Death wasn't afraid of that Old Dog Shuck. He knew that he just to reach out his hand and Old Shuck would be struck just as dead as graveyard dirt. A single puff of Old Man Death's freezer-cold breath would have iced the very flesh of Shuck from off of his old dog bones – but Old Man Death truly admired the courage that the old dog was showing."

"That's an awfully good dog you've got there boy – Old Man Death said to Little Billy," Coyote went on. "And while he was saying that he blew just enough of his breath onto Little Billy just enough for that fever up and stepped straight out of Little Billy's bones quicker than you could say spit on a stick."

Coyote kept on talking and I just followed him right on inside that story until I might as well have been standing there on Little Billy's front porch right directly next to Coyote – the two of us listening to what Old Man Death had to say.

"Do you think that you would sell that dog to me?" Old Man Death asked. "I'd sure like to have him as my own."

"Well that depends on what you want to pay for him," Little Billy replied. "I'm kind of thinking that nothing you offer is going to be enough. Right now Old Shuck is all I have left of my family."

"The price is your life," Old Man Death said. "If that dog comes with me than you have to got to get up and shake this fever from out of your bones and live to about a hundred and three years of age – give or take a day or two."

Little Billy didn't know what to say – but Old Shuck knew exactly what needed to be done.

"That dog walked right on up to Old Man Death and he licked Death's bony fingers with his long pink tongue," Coyote kept on talking. "And the salt of the dead man's bones worked its way into Old Shuck's bloodstream and right then and right there he became Death's very own dog."

"So I guess that Death sweat works just a little bit like Giant Tears do," I said, thinking back to Old Nanna Bijou, back in Thunder Bay – laying in a pool of his own tears and slowly turning into a mountain.

"I guess it does," Coyote agreed with a knowing grin. "Just a little bit."

And then Coyote slid right back into his story.

"So when ever Old Man Death knows that he has to make himself a house call," Coyote went on telling. "He sends Old Shuck ahead to let people know that it's time to go. Old Shuck is what some folks call a psychopomp – a messenger of Death. It was Old Shuck's job to let families know that it is time for the saying of goodbyes. He lets people know when they have to go and make casserole and when they have to get their church clothes cleaned and pressed. He lets people know that Old Man Death is coming close behind."

I shivered just a little.

Coyote smiled like that shiver was what he had been trying for in the first place.

He winked at me and Bigfoot grinned and just exactly before I giggled out loud when I realized just how scared silly I had really been – the grandfather of all hound dogs barked outside The Prophet's door.

"It sounds like we've got company," Bigfoot said, with a grin.

"Let's just pretend that we're not home," Coyote suggested. "It's probably just a salesman looking to sell us some toilet brushes."

But of course Bigfoot did not listen to Coyote's suggestion.

Instead, he got up and opened the door.

It wasn't Death at the door – and it wasn't a traveling toilet brush salesman. It was something a whole lot worse than either of those two combined.

It was Old Shuck.

He had heard Coyote tell his story told and Old Shuck had come running.

As big as life and twice as ugly.

Chapter Twenty – Death Dog Beat Down

CAN YOU JUST try and picture a pit bull crossed with a purple hippopotamus?

"I hate dogs," Bigfoot growled. "Especially big purple ones."

Then once you've got that purple pit bull hippo successfully crossed throw in a mouth full of teeth that sort of looked like they were carved out enamel-coated mountain peaks. Add a hide full of muscle and whale-meat, a set of eyebrows that looked as if they needed to watered and mowed regularly.

Then throw in a heavy handed helping of all-around size and enough of a body mass so that picture basically needs its very own postal code.

Now you're getting the idea of what Old Shuck REALLY looked like.

"What's wrong with dogs?" Coyote asked, sounding a little hurt. "I mean, besides the big and the mean and all those teeth?"

Old Shuck growled right back.

He didn't sound as if Bigfoot's growling had intimidated him one little bit.

"Dogs are two-faced," Bigfoot said. "One moment they are all wagging tail and loll-the-tongue – but you forget to feed them their dinner and the wolf-memory creeps on in and all of a sudden it's a WHOLE different kind of story."

Old Shuck growled a little bit louder.

"Do you know what I figure?" I asked aloud to no one in particular. "I think that Old Shuck has just figured out that whole dinner problem – and I am pretty sure that we are it!"

Old Shuck growled again.

I think he might have been agreeing with me.

"I want you to distract him," Bigfoot told Coyote. "Then I'll make my move."

"How about if you make your move first and I'll just stand here and act distracted," Coyote replied. "I'm awfully good at acting distracted."

Meanwhile, Old Shuck just sat there looking about as B-I-G as a giant purple hippo dog could look.

Let me tell you, he was awfully good at that too.

In fact, in addition to his own postal code I think that dog might have had a gravitational field of his very own.

"I don't want you to catch him," Bigfoot told Coyote. "I just want you to sort of flush him out — not that you'd know all that much about flushing."

"Is there anything I can do?" I asked, trying to step back enough to put the two of them between me and that garage-sized canine."

"So how good are you at staying out of the way?" Bigfoot asked.

"What do you mean?"

"I mean just shut up, stand there and do nothing," Bigfoot said. "Okay?"

That hurt my feelings a bit — but I guess I really couldn't blame him. After all, he was the expert monster fighter.

I was just some little kid.

What the heck could I do?

Nothing.

"I can do that," I said – even though it hurt to say it. "You want me to do nothing than that's just exactly what I will do."

"I am still waiting for you to explain that wisecrack about me not flushing," Coyote complained to Bigfoot. "I'll have you know that we coyotes are by nature true and total masters of simple basic hygiene."

"Maybe so," Bigfoot allowed. "But your toilet habits leave a WHOLE lot to be desired – or do you REALLY imagine that your beneath-the-tail tastes anything remotely like sugar plums and sweet butter?"

By about this point Old Shuck had got bored with our company. He stood up – which was a little like watching a Greyhound bus grow its own set of legs and wag its tailpipe – and then he wandered over to a clump of trees and began delicately anointing them with a dirty gentle lemonade.

Yes sir – for a giant purple dog, Old Shuck definitely had class.

"All right mangy foot," Bigfoot said to Coyote. "Here's what we'll do. You run into that thicket of jack pines and flush him out like I told you to. You head him my way and I'll jump on him as he goes running past me."

"What about me?" The Prophet asked. "I want to help too."

"How are you at shutting up, Winnie?" Bigfoot asked. "You just park yourself right where you are at and I will let you know when we need something."

"That wasn't a very nice thing to say," The Prophet said.

I kind of half-agreed with The Prophet – that WASN'T a very nice thing for Bigfoot to have said to The Prophet.

"No one ever said that I was especially nice," Bigfoot said. "Now you just do what I told you and you sit there and shut the heck up."

So that's just what the Prophet did – but I am pretty certain that giant pink flying Winnebago was sulking as well – and I was pretty sure I saw a few streaks of windshield washer fluid tearing up around the corners of his front windshield – and I guess I couldn't blame him if he really was crying.

Bigfoot had been awfully rough on him after all.

I knew just what he felt like.

"Do you have any intelligent suggestions on just how I am supposed to aim that big purple dog in any other direction other than the one he feels like going in?" Coyote asked. "Providing he doesn't take it into his wedge-shaped head to run directly at me?"

"That's exactly what I am counting on," Bigfoot said. "You just get him running at you and then I'll surprise him from behind."

"Just once," Coyote grumbled. "Just freaking once I would like to take a shot at that whole surprising from behind department."

"That's my particular area of expertise," Bigfoot pointed out. "You are sort of good at running and I am very good at surprising – ESPECIALLY from behind."

So Coyote went on in to flush the Death Dog out of the jack pine thicket.

He kind of sneaked up on Old Shuck.

I'm not quite sure how he did it. One moment he was sitting there beside us and the very next he had sort of moved on and blended into the shadows of the pine trees.

"I will give him that," Bigfoot said to me. "Mangy or not, that Coyote is as stealthy as all get out."

By now Old Shuck had completely vanished into that thicket of jack pine faster than a playing card at a magician's convention. I am guessing that Coyote was still following him but I couldn't really be sure because by then he was completely invisible.

The plan was working – which, in hindsight, was ALWAYS a bad sign.

All at once Old Shuck came charging out of that thicket of jack pines baying in a voice so loud and deep and cranky that it sounded as if somebody had dropped a rusted-out iron woodstove down a three hundred foot coal mine shaft about four or five thousand times in a row.

I am talking deep-down thunder-yelling, earthquake-rumbling, kettle drum demolitions.

The big old death-dog sounded as if he had swallowed a tribe full of motorcycles and had spit out each of the mufflers.

Coyote was running close behind the death-dog.

In fact, Coyote had hold of Old Shuck's tail.

I could see him hanging on as Old Shuck ran straight past us.

Coyote was stuck straight out in the wind like Old Shuck had gone and grown himself his very own fur-covered flea-bitten exhaust pipe.

"GEE-RON-AH-HOO-HAW!" Bigfoot shouted, leaping straight up into the air like he was part-kangaroo and part rocket-powered pogo stick. He landed on top of the death dog – with his arms and his legs spread wide as if he were attempting to straddle the Grand Canyon and a half.

Yes sir, I have got to give credit to that Sasquatch.

He was definitely big on offence.

He looked pretty darned impressive but judging from the way that Old Shuck took his weight in stride he was having no more effect on that big old death dog than a piece of dandelion fluff alighting upon the left antler of a three billion year old bull moose.

However, Bigfoot's distraction did give Coyote a chance to shift his grip a little and to bite down even harder on Old Shuck's tail – which worked just fine until Old Shuck took it into his head to sit down.

Right directly on top of Coyote.

It did make an awfully interesting sound – when that big black death-dog's bottom end squashed down on top of Coyote's all-over end. It kind of sounded a little like the world's largest nuclear amoeba splashing down upon a Godzilla-sized water balloon.

I'm not saying that it sounded pretty.

Still, the fact that Old Shuck was now sitting directly upon Coyote did not seem to bother Bigfoot one little bit. In fact, it almost seemed to cheer him up. He hammered the death dog about three or four times with the side of his big hairy fist before Old Shuck performed a most amazing sort of a maneuver that went sort of like this.

On the fifth time that Bigfoot hauled one of his big hairy fists back, Old Shuck turned and opened his mouth and when Bigfoot swung he hit nothing but a set of wide open death dog jaws. His arm sort of slid elbow-deep down into Old Shuck's mouth.

"Can you hold him like that?" I asked.

"I'm not sure who's actually doing the holding," Bigfoot admitted, swinging his other big hairy fist down again. "It's either him or me, I guess."

"Aim for a molar!" I suggested.

Old Shuck closed his mouth down even harder on Bigfoot's arm. I couldn't tell if he was chewing or not.

"I think I found that molar you were talking about," Bigfoot said. "Only it might be somewhere sunk into my right arm wrist bone."

It sure didn't look good for our side.

Bigfoot was trapped elbow-deep in Old Shuck's mouth.

Coyote was busy being squashed.

And then the big death dog began to slurp.

FLOOP!

Bigfoot slid into the big dog's mouth just a little further. It was a little like watching a very fat man slurp down a very large strand of spaghetti – except it wasn't a fat man doing the slurping - it was a big fat dog. And it wasn't a strand of spaghetti that it was slurping.

It was the right arm of a Cape Breton Bigfoot.

Bigfoot did his very best to resist the big dog's irresistible suction, using his free left arm to hammer on the right side of Old Shuck's head but Old Shuck just ignored the hammering and inhaled again.

FLOOP!

Bigfoot's arm disappeared even deeper into Old Shuck's mouth; only by now Bigfoot was buried up to his shoulder in dog mouth.

"Okay," Bigfoot said. "This REALLY sucks."

And then Old Shuck inhaled again.

FLOOP!

It would have been funny, if I hadn't been so terrified.

Bigfoot's head was buried completely inside of Old Shuck's mouth.

He looked a little like a lion tamer stuck in permanent epic fail mode.

"Hum-mum-um-num-um-num," Bigfoot said - which sounded an awful lot like "I'm stuck. Get me out of here before he decides to chew."

Which was followed by another swallow.

FLOOP!

It wasn't too hard to see where this going to end up.

A couple of more swallows and Bigfoot was going to discover the hidden secrets of canine digestion – from the inside out.

Old Shuck was going to swallow Bigfoot whole.

I turned and I ran.

Straight for the mystical pink Winnebago.

Chapter Twenty One – Me, Doing Something

JUST SHUT UP and and stand there and do nothing was exactly what Bigfoot had told me to do – but I had to do something.

So to start with I ran for the big pink Winnebago. I opened the door, jumped in and then I slammed the door behind me.

"Hey!" the Prophet shouted. "Easy on the paint job."

Only I wasn't all that worried about his paint job.

"Bigfoot is in trouble," I said. "So is Coyote."

That didn't seem to impress the Prophet one little bit.

"I'm sorry," he said. "But you must be mistaking me for somebody who might actually give a hydro-electric beaver dam."

"They are your friends, aren't they?" I asked. "I heard you say that very thing, right out loud, not too long ago."

"Maybe you ought to get your ears cleaned out." The Prophet replied. "I think you might have misheard something somewhere along the way."

I guess that he was still upset over what Bigfoot had said to him – but I wasn't going to give up on trying to convince him to think differently.

"THEY'RE YOUR FRIENDS!" I shouted.

"WHO FREAKING CARES?" The Prophet shouted back.

He blared that last sentence at the top of his Magic Winnebago lungs – which were awfully freaking loud. In fact, he blared that last sentence so very freaking loudly that I am pretty sure that his blaring had left big fat purple bruises in the back of my eardrums.

"Friends don't hurt each other's feelings," the Prophet went on. "Friends don't leave friends out of the action. And friends don't call other friends WINNIE!"

I couldn't believe what he was telling me.

"Are you kidding me?" I asked. "Bigfoot is practically your brother and Coyote – well, he is almost like a sister to you, now isn't he?"

The Prophet thought about that.

"I had a brother once," he said. "His name was Tecumseh. Maybe you've heard about him. He had a whole lot to do with Canada winning the War of 1812."

I knew that The Prophet had something to tell me. I knew it was something that he felt he had to get out of his system before he could get around to even thinking about helping Bigfoot and the Coyote. I even knew that I had to keep my mouth shut just long enough for him to tell me his story and then we could maybe get on with it.

But that didn't mean that I had to like it.

"He sounds like a really good guy," I said, trying to kid him along into agreeing with me. "Your brother, I mean. Tecumseh."

A part of me wished that it was Tecumseh who was here to help us right now – rather than his brother, The Prophet.

"Tecumseh was a REALLY good guy," The Prophet said. "Everyone said so. That was the whole problem. Nobody really ever seemed to notice me. It was always Tecumseh this and Tecumseh that. He was always the handsome one and he was the brave one and he was the one that everyone listened to."

Are you freaking kidding me?

I had heard just as much of this story as I could put up with.

"ARE YOU FREAKING STUPID OR SOMETHING?" I shouted. "BIGFOOT IS GETTING EATEN BY A GIANT PURPLE DOG AND YOU ARE SITTING IN HERE HOLDING YOURSELF A GIANT PURPLE PRIVATE PITY PARTY?"

"You don't understand," The Prophet began to explain. "That isn't how it was."

Only I wasn't going to put up with one minute more of his cry baby explaining.

There was a time for a talking and a time for just doing SOMETHING!

"OH BOO-HOO, BOO-HOO, BOO-HOO-DE-DOO-HOO," I went on, just as loud and sarcastic as I could get. "POOR ME. NOBODY LOVES ME. POOR, POOR LITTLE OLD ME. EVERYBODY LOVES TECUMSEH. NOBODY LOVES ME."

"Yeah? Is that so?" The Prophet asked right back at me. "I guess you wouldn't know a thing about holding regular private pity parties – would you mister-my-Dad-has-died-and-I-don't-know-what-to-do-about-it?"

At which point The Prophet opened all of his doors – even the refrigerator door.

"You can get out and walk home anytime that you like," The Prophet told me. "If you're going to shout at me like you've been doing."

I couldn't believe what I was hearing.

He wasn't budging.

Coyote and Bigfoot were being swallowed by a giant blue amoeba death-dog – and this reincarnated Shawnee holy man was stuck on a few hurt feelings.

I had to do something.

But what?

So I came around from another direction and I decided to hit him with an unexpected heartfelt apology – even if I didn't really feel much sorry for him at the time.

"All right," I said. "I'm sorry. I didn't mean to yell at you."

I'm sorry doesn't always cut it – but sometimes a simple heart-felt apology will go a long way towards settling any particular dispute.

The Prophet wobbled his doors a little and let his engine run a little softer, like he was thinking about what I was saying.

"So what happened to him?" I asked. "Your brother, I mean."

The engine came to a full stop.

I sat there and I waited.

There wasn't anything else that I could do.

"He died," The Prophet finally said. "At a battle outside of a little place called Moraviantown. Even then he was a big man. He had to make a big deal out of EVERYTHING he did. He even shook the hand of each one of the British soldiers before he marched into a swamp. He was shot in the chest, defending that swamp. What a lousy reason to die – over a stinking lousy piece of swampland."

I saw a few more sad streaks of windshield fluid running down the front of his windshield. The big old Winnebago shook a little – rocking on his suspension and I guess that was his way of sobbing.

I heard a bird singing overhead.

I let that bird sing on a little while The Prophet just sat there and sobbed and stewed in his own juices.

"All this time," The Prophet went on. "I just wish I could have a chance to tell him I am truly sorry for what happened. I wish that

I could have a chance to help him do EXACTLY what he was trying to do."

Finally I knew just what I had to say.

"You told me that you're my friend, now didn't you?" I asked, trying very hard not to shout. "I didn't mishear that, now did I?"

The Prophet ground his gears just a little in a show of frustration.

"What?" I asked. "Don't you have any answer for me?"

That brought on a little more gear-grinding.

He spun his wheels a little bit in the mud.

Then underneath all of that gear-grinding and wheel spinning I heard five tiny words, barely beeped out.

"Yes," The Prophet said. "You ARE my friend."

"Well - friends don't ever let their friends down," I said, trying very hard not to raise my voice. There was a time for getting mad and there was a time for getting your own way done. "I asked you for help. You told me no. You told me to get out and walk."

I didn't even bother mentioning that I was a HECK of a long way away from my home.

"They are my friends," I said. "And you are my friend. And you need to help me help my friends, my friend."

I think I might have sprained my tongue on those last three or four sentences but it seemed to do the trick.

For a moment The Prophet just sat there saying nothing.

I sat there saying nothing right along with him.

I didn't even dare breathe.

For all either of us knew Bigfoot and Coyote had already been swallowed by that giant purple death dog.

And then all at once The Prophet slammed ALL of his doors at once – including the fridge door – which shocked me right back into breathing – not to mention almost catching my finger in mid-slam – where I had been quietly reaching for a can of grape soda.

"Well?" I asked.

"Get in and drive," The Prophet said. "My friends are in trouble."

"You want me to drive?"

"Somebody has to drive," The Prophet said. "It is the way that the magic works."

I nervously sat behind the steering wheel.

"Squeeze that steering wheel just a little," The Prophet told me. "And then lean in just as far as you are able to."

I squeezed the wheel. I felt it squeeze back just a little. It felt as if the wheel were made out of some magic sort of super-sticky fly paper. I felt it pull me in, just a little – like The Prophet was trying to swallow me whole.

For just a half of an instant I was scared that The Prophet was still angry and that he would swallow me and then all three of us – me, Bigfoot and Coyote – would be stuck out here in the backwoods of nowhere-at-all-in-particular. Maybe years later some archeologist would stumble in here and somehow dig up my remains half-buried in the steering wheel of a giant pink magic Winnebago travel home – and then he'd write a paper on how my Batman backpack somehow caused the extinction of the dinosaurs.

"Don't be afraid," The Prophet told me. "Just push in a little bit with your imagination and then let her rip."

So I pushed.

I felt that steering wheel pull me in like it was made out of sped-up quicksand. I felt the spirit of that great mystical pink Winnebago wash over me and then all at once I was grinning through the steel and chrome bumper and squinting out of the big machine's headlights.

And then the Prophet let it rip.

Chapter Twenty Two – The Prophet to the Rescue, Sort Of

HAVE YOU EVER heard the sound of a jet plane getting set to take off? Do you know how the roaring noise will build and build and build until it feels as if your ears had been poured full of screaming sacred sea monkeys?

The sound that The Prophet was making was way louder than that.

The Prophet took off with me holding on to the steering wheel for dear sweet life.

I know that I was supposed to be driving. I know that was how The Prophet's magic actually worked – but that didn't help one single bit from me feeling like I was nothing more than a horsefly glued feet-first to the top end of a speeding locomotive speeding along on a railroad built straight down the mouth of the Grand Canyon.

The engine was roaring out loud. The wheels were spinning like crazy souped-up hamster wheels. Trees crashed to the ground and I am pretty sure that one or two of them actually uprooted themselves and hiked their bark up around their knotty old kneecaps as they scampered for cover.

Old Shuck got about half of a blink's worth of time to see us coming straight directly at his big purple squatty old self.

And then we hit – the three of us – me, in a giant pink Winnebago ramming smack-dab into the middle of a giant purple Death Dog.

Now why don't you try telling me just how many times in your life you might expect to use a sentence like THAT???

We made a sound like we had just hit the world's largest rubber super ball bouncing hard against Old Shuck's grape-colored hide. It was a little like hitting a gigantic elastic band. Old Shuck's body sort of stretched in and around the oncoming magical Winnebago. The big death dog made a soft wet what-the-freak sort of sound as he spit Bigfoot out into thin mid-air.

Bigfoot hit the windshield of the Winnebago and he sort of flattened out across it like the shadow of a thin and runny steam-rolled fur-pancake. Bigfoot's eyes were about as wide as giant Frisbees and his lips smeared against The Prophet's windshield, leaving long slug-like tracks of Bigfoot spit smeared across the window glass.

I'm not saying it was pretty.

"HANG ON!" The Prophet roared.

I'm not sure if The Prophet was talking to me – or if he was actually talking to Bigfoot who was still hanging off of the windshield, trying his hardest not to die.

It might be he was even talking to himself.

"LET GO OF MY FREAKING WIPER BLADE!" The Prophet roared. "YOU BIG STUPID HAIRY WANNABE-WOOKIE!"

That time I was pretty sure that he was DEFINITELY talking to Bigfoot.

We powered straight ahead, driving directly into Old Shuck.

"We're going to flatten him out like a toad in the road," I yelled.

Only I guess it didn't work that way with giant purple Death Dogs.

The deeper we drove into Old Shuck's body, the more his body stretched out – until we were driving into nothing but a sea of deep rubber purple. It was like that Death Dog was made up of some kind of a giant elastic amoeba. I began to worry that he was going to swallow us up inside of himself and then crawl off into some deep and funky cave to hibernate while he digested about five tons of mystical pink Winnebago along with the spirit of a reincarnated Shawnee medicine man, a nine foot tall Sasquatch, a Coyote trickster and a seventeen year old boy.

Namely, me.

"I am Tenskwatawa," The Prophet roared defiantly. "I am the brother to the mighty Tecumseh. I am the Open Door and I am the Arrow – and you, tiny little purple funny-smelling dog must yield before my power!"

Well that sounded all right when you roared it through a mystical pink Winnebago bumper – but it just did not seem to impress Old Shuck all that much.

In the heart of the deep purple forever that Old Shuck had grown and stretched into – something went *SPROINGGGGGGG!!!*

It sounded as if King Kong had jumped upon a pogo stick deep in the belly of Moby Dick – while old Moby was swimming through the bottom basement level of the Marianas Trench, trying to digest the Olympic-sized trampoline that he had recently swallowed. I felt my bones and my body wobble like they were made out of half-chilled purple Jell-O.

And then we snapped on back.

The last thing I saw was Bigfoot bouncing backwards off of The Prophet's windshield and right back down into Old Shuck's windpipe while we were simultaneously flinging backwards at about a thousand and a half miles an hour. It happened just like one of those cartoons when somebody runs into a giant rubber band and then suddenly snaps back.

We snapped directly back through the woods of Nova Scotia. I saw the Atlantic Ocean splash below us like a rain puddle seen from the top of a tree. We flashed over Europe, straight through

France – which I could tell because I caught a very brief glimpse of the Eifel Tower.

I saw something else too.

Just as we passed over Nova Scotia I looked down and I saw a search party hunting through the Cape Breton woods – looking for me and Warren, I guess. I'm not exactly sure just how it was that I spotted that tiny little detail out of all of that landscape that was flashing on past. It might have been some sort of magic, it might have been just pure dumb luck – heck, it might have been I made the whole thing up in my imagination.

I saw it and then it was gone.

Meanwhile, we kept on gaining altitude.

Little details kept popping out at me.

I saw a flight of snowy white Norwegian storks go migrating past, in reverse

Over Russia, I saw an SU-25 Frogfoot close support aircraft – and don't ask me how I knew what sort of a plane it was because I just KNEW was all - whip past us for just long enough for the Russian pilot to shake his head in complete and utter disbelief.

I figured that any moment now I was most likely going to see angel wings – and maybe they'd be attached to me.

I could feel a tickle of polar fear crawling up and down my spinal column like a drunken parade of centipedes wearing ice cubes in place of shoes.

And then all of a sudden everything got quiet and still. Do you know that feeling when your ears pop and sound sort of drowns itself out for just a half of a half of a second? Well, it was just like that – only I had the feeling that the ears of the whole wide world had just collectively and simultaneously popped.

And just for that single half of a half of a half second I could swear that I could hear somebody talking.

It was Warren.

He said to me – "Don't you worry, Adam. Everything is going to work out just fine. Just you wait and see."

And then my ears re-popped and I blinked really hard and everything was back to the way it had been – and I can't even tell you if the whole thing really happened.

By that time we had reached the Himalayas and those huge goat-peaked mountains looked like nothing more than herd of poorly-maintained speed bumps.

"All right," The Prophet yelled out. "That's far enough!"

We screamed a huge hairpin U-turn around an orbiting satellite, knocking the television reception out of the state of Hawaii as we laid a white-water speed trail directly across the entire left half of the southern Pacific Ocean.

At the height of our flight I saw a fully-grown comet shoot past.

"Did you see that?" I asked – looking at the comet.

"Did I see what?" the Prophet asked, looking at something else.

I guess he was too busy achieving a near supersonic velocity to bother looking around or listening to the seventeen year old boy who was spiritually inhabiting the vicinity of his headlights – but I swore that I saw the Raven riding on top of that high-flying comet – grinning directly at me and laughing like he was watching the most funniest thing that he had ever witnessed in the whole wide world.

That might have been my imagination too – only I'm pretty sure it wasn't.

"Hold onto your seat-bone," the Prophet warned. "Things may get a little rough."

We roared back into Nova Scotia.

The pine trees blinked past like the shadow-spokes of a bicycle wheel spun against the sunrise. I was stuck there in the headlights of The Prophet, pretty certain that we were going to plow into the Nova Scotia landscape like a poorly driven meteorite.

And then everything slowed down, all at once.

"You can get back up now," the Prophet said.

I leaned back and I felt myself rising up from out of the spiritual essence of that giant pink Winnebago, like I was rising up out of the deep end of a lukewarm swimming pool.

I was sitting in the driver's seat and the steering wheel unpuckered itself from the squeeze of my grip like a hand stuck full of dried maple syrup.

I stepped out and we were back where we had started from.

We were back in Nova Scotia.

The only thing that had changed was that Old Shuck had Bigfoot swallowed right down to his ankles.

All I could see was a pair of big fat furry feet sticking out from between that big purple dog's lips.

"You want me to take another run at him?" The Prophet asked. "I think I softened him up the first time."

He was game to try it again, but I shook my head no.

"That didn't work before," I said, letting go of the steering wheel and stepping back out of the Prophet. "I think I am going to try something different."

I untangled myself up from the driver's seat.

Then I walked to the door and I stepped on outside of the giant pink Winnebago.

And then I walked right up towards Old Shuck.

"Hey Shuck," I said. "Good dog. Good old dog."

Old Shuck looked at me like I was wearing two heads – and both of them were made out of freshly-cooked pot roast.

Unfortunately, I wasn't really sure if he wasn't right.

Don't worry – the voice of Warren kind of ghost-repeated itself in the back of my ears somewhere behind my imagination and just left of my sense of wonder – everything is going to be all right.

I sure hoped that Warren's ghost voice knew exactly what it was talking about.

Chapter Twenty Three – Hair of the Dog

"**GOOD DOG,**" I said, making old maiden aunt sounds. "Yes you are, yes you really are - Old Shuck is a good, good dog."

I wished for a rubber ball – or even just a good-sized hand grenade.

Old Shuck just kept on staring at me as if I were wearing a set of freshly-ground hamburger pants. I figured that he had already had most of Bigfoot as a main course and now he was considering me as a possible dessert to have after he had finished his Bigfoot banquet.

But I had to try and do something.

"Good Shuck," I said. "Good Old Shuck."

"Mmmphbubshumrumahbuan…" Coyote mumbled from underneath Old Shuck's mighty purple hind end.

"Would you mind subtitling that?" I asked. "Or at the very least you could try mumbling a little bit louder."

Coyote wiggled his mouth just free enough underneath of the heavy purple dog butt to make himself heard.

"I said that his full name is Shukramarama," Coyote suggested. "Remember, like in the story I told you?"

Old Shuck's ears perked up at the sound of that name, just a little.

Of course, he might have had a flea or a tick or a nuclear bore-worm nibbling on his left lower ear lobe – but I took that ear perk to be a good sign.

"Good dog," I repeated. "Good old Shukramarama."

Old Shuck grinned a little – one of those big and happy dog grins that just naturally makes you want to reach down and skritch his ears.

Which I did.

I wasn't all that happy about skritching his ears but I figured that if I was going to have any sort of a chance of actually rescuing Bigfoot – this was it.

I skritched those big purple ears really good, working my fingers into each skritch. His hide felt thick – the sort of thick of a walrus hide – or at the very least what I imagined a walrus hide would feel like – if I ever got close enough to a walrus to skritch one.

Old Shuck started to thump his big old purple tail happily.

"Ouch," Coyote mumbled.

And then Old Shuck made the kind of dog sound that you don't EVER want to hear your own dog making. Faster than you could say "What elephant died in this garbage can", a weird funky odor that smelled a little bit like a road-killed landfill drifted up from the vicinity of Old Shuck's big thumping tail.

Meaning he farted.

"Shoot me," Coyote pathetically whimpered from below Old Shuck's thumping funky tail. "Somebody just please shoot me now."

"Good dog," I repeated, trying my best not to choke upon the penetrating reek of Old Shuck's way-past-foul dog farts. "Good old Shukramarama."

I saw that Bigfoot's feet seemed to be sticking out just a little further from Old Shuck's mouth – so I guess maybe my skritching was relaxing Old Shuck's mouth grip.

"Are you still alive in there?" I asked.

Bigfoot must have heard me asking, because he wiggled his big fuzzy toes just as frantically as was possible.

"You might want to give thanks that he has already swallowed your nostrils," I said. "The funking farty reek is awfully penetrating out here."

That was right about the time when I felt what seemed to be a long smooth snake slithering slowly over my left ankle.

I looked down and I saw that The Prophet had quietly unspooled a long pink metal cable from a hidden winch that appeared to be connected to a spot located somewhere beneath his front bumper.

"Good dog," I repeated for the third time. "Good old Shukramarama."

I knelt down and I picked up the cable and then I tied as solid of a knot as I could – looping the cable around both of Bigfoot's big hairy ankles.

It wasn't anything remotely close to a Turkish half and a half hitch reef dragon-tying knot but I did the best that I could, pausing every now and then for another good dog, good Shukramarama and a couple of more heart-felt head-skritches.

"What's going on out there?" Coyote mumble-asked from beneath Old Shuck's bottom end. "I can't see a single thing."

"Can you drive yourself in reverse?" I carefully called back over my shoulder to The Prophet. "Is that possible?"

"Not without anyone at the wheel," The Prophet replied. "That's not how the magic works."

I was getting awfully tired of hearing him tell me that.

Did he expect me to do EVERYTHING for him?

"Well can you roll this cable back up by yourself?" I asked patiently. "Is that doable?"

"I can do that." The Prophet said.

"Well, be ready," I said. "And roll fast."

I reached down and I picked up a stick, leaned back and in one motion hurled that piece of pine branch about as far out into the woods as I could manage to throw it.

"FETCH!" I shouted.

Now I would have looked like ten miles of a long stupid road if Old Shuck hadn't gone and done what I had hoped he would go and do – but he went ahead and did it.

He sort of made a determined two foot punch from off of the flattest portion of Coyote's head, opening his mouth wide in an honest display of pure canine happiness.

And as he opened his mouth I yelled "PULL!" and then The Prophet started reeling that magic retractable winch cable right back on in.

Bigfoot came out of Old Shuck's wide open big purple mouth like a nine foot long strand of furry unwashed spaghetti in reverse.

He arced skyward, looking a little like a big furry salmon jumping from out of a deep purple stream, banshee-howling as he jumped. Then he landed with a big furry ka-thump at my feet, looked up at me once and blinked hard twice before The Prophet reeled him in – only knocking over two stumps and three trees on his way back to the mystic pink travel home.

"Ouch," said Coyote, slowly getting to his feet. "I bet that hurt him a whole lot worse than it hurt me."

At that point Old Shuck galloped back towards me, spit the pine stick out into the dirt at my feet and licked my face clean with his long purple tongue.

At which point I leaned over into a nearby sugarplum bush and emptied out about half of what was left of my breakfast.

Followed shortly by the other half.

I'm not saying it was pretty – but at least it smelled a whole lot better than Old Shuck's horrifying butt-funk gas.

But not by much.

Chapter Twenty Four – Word Choice is Awfully Important

BIGFOOT HELD THE bearskin beneath Old Shuck's mighty purple nose.

From where I was standing that bearskin smelled a little like the leftover breakfast that I had just emptied out of my stomach and into the sugar plum bushes a short time ago – but Old Shuck seemed to like it just fine.

"Come on you big purple Barney dog," Bigfoot said. "Come on and get yourself a really good snoot full."

The big purple death dog snorted the bear pelt daintily.

And then he sneezed about a bucket and a half full of giant green and purple dog snot all over Bigfoot.

"Maybe he is allergic to you," Coyote suggested. "I have heard of such things."

"It might help if you actually used his real name," I added. "Rather than calling him Barney. He really doesn't look a thing like that big purple television dinosaur."

Bigfoot wasn't impressed by my suggestion.

"Maybe he's actually allergic to stupidity," Bigfoot replied. "How about if you two stand back up and let this big fellow breathe?"

"Listen to the fur ball talk," The Prophet said. "I'm betting that big old Sasquatch couldn't even SPELL the word allergic if he had it written out in front of his eyeballs."

Honestly, I wasn't even sure if I could spell allergic without using a "k" or two – but I didn't bother saying so. I was way too busy watching the effect that bewitched bear pelt seemed to have on Old Shuck.

He growled at that Spirit Bear pelt.

"I don't think he likes the smell of that bear pelt all that much," Coyote said.

"I don't care WHAT he likes," Bigfoot said. "He is a hunting dog and that means that he is supposed to be able to hunt."

Old Shuck put his big purple paw over his head, like he didn't want to listen to what ever Bigfoot had to say.

Bigfoot grabbed Old Shuck by his ear and held his face up close to his own – close enough to either lick or bite, which I thought was quite a risk. Then he shoved the bear skin back under the big purple dog's nose.

"Fetch!" Bigfoot said.

Old Shuck growled a little deeper in his throat.

"I don't think that grabbing onto his ear is all that good of an idea," Coyote pointed out. "He doesn't really seem to like it all that much."

"Here, kid," Bigfoot said – holding the spirit bear's pelt in my direction. "You seem to have better luck with this Death Dog than I do."

"It might be because Adam behaves a whole lot nicer than you do," Coyote pointed out. "Did you ever stop and think of that?"

"If I want to hear from you I'll pull your tail like a bell rope," Bigfoot warned. "And you can just say ding."

"Like I said," Coyote added, tucking his tail under all four of his feet. "A whole lot nicer than you know how."

I held the bear skin in my hands like it was a peed-on blanket that had been forgotten behind somebody's bed and left to grow mildew.

And then I stepped a little closer.

"Hey Old Shuck," I said. "Old Shuckster, good old Shukramarama."

Old Shuck panted happily and thumped his tail in the dirt, rising up a dust cloud about the size and density of Vancouver Island squared fourteen times a hundred.

He really seemed to like me.

I knew what was happening.

You'd have to be ten kinds of stupid not to recognize what Shukramarama was really looking at when he saw me.

He was seeing Little Billy standing there – the boy that Old Shuck had died for. He was seeing Little Billy as a kid again, and ready to play.

That was fine by me. The truth was I had begun to grow a big old soft spot, right directly in the center of my heart for this ugly purple Death Dog. If he wanted me to be his Little Billy – well that was fine as fine could be.

"Sniff on this," I told Old Shuck. "Come on boy."

Old Shuck took himself a sniff.

He panted happily, big purple gobs of dog-drool hanging down his big fuzzy chin.

Then he took himself another big old sniff.

Then he barked.

"I think he's got the scent," Bigfoot said happily. "What did I tell you? That was easy. I knew the kid could do it."

I rolled my eyes a little.

"Shut up and the let the kid do his work and stop trying to take the credit for something you had no idea would happen," Coyote growled. "Adam knows exactly what he's doing."

I smiled at that.

"Come on Old Shuck," I said, shaking the pelt of the Spirit Bear. "Fetch now, fetch!"

Old Shuck opened his purple garbage truck mouth and took the pelt away from me and then he spat the pelt back down at my feet.

He looked up and panted happily, wagging his tail and waiting patiently for another skritch.

I guess that proper word choice when dealing with a giant purple Death Dog can be AWFULLY important.

"You fetched it all right," I said, giving him the reward of his waited-for head skritch. "Good old Shuck, good old Shuckaramarama."

"It might be you want to rephrase your command," Coyote suggested. "Remember – good grammar is the difference between "Let's eat Granddad" and "Let's eat, Granddad.""

"Yeah, and it might be that you just might like to take your own advice for yourself," Bigfoot added. "And just shut up for a bit and let the kid do his stuff."

So I picked up the Spirit Bear pelt, and I gave it another shake and carefully held it back under Old Shuck's nose.

Old Shuck gave another big old sniff.

"All right Old Shuck," I said. "Good old Shuckeramarama."

I thought very carefully about what I was going to say next.

And then it came to me.

I don't think that I thought of it, actually. It was more like I heard someone inside of my brain whispering the word to me - somebody that sounded a whole lot like my stepdad Warren.

I knew the three words that I had to say.

I gave Old Shuck another sniff of Spirit Bear – and then I said those three words.

"Let's go hunting," I said.

Old Shuck barked happily and then took off running.

The hunt was on.

"Let's go," Bigfoot yelled.

We climbed into The Prophet and took off with a beat of his mighty pink wings – and we took off following directly behind Old Shuck from high above.

I could see him running down below, from my window seat. He looked like a giant fat grape-colored tick, bouncing through the woodland.

"He's almost to the shoreline," Coyote said. "I sure he hope he can swim."

"He'll most likely dog paddle," Bigfoot replied.

Only it turned out that Old Shuck did not need to swim.

He reached the water and then he just kept on running, like the Atlantic Ocean was nothing more than a great big playground.

"How does he do that?" I asked.

"Magic would be my guess," Bigfoot said.

"The next time you're talking to that big purple dog," Coyote suggested. "Why don't you try asking him just exactly how he does it?"

We followed – flying above Old Shuck for about an hour.

We had flown practically halfway across the Gulf of St. Lawrence and were heading for the Labrador coastline when the Raven decided to attack.

Chapter Twenty Five – Wayward Sky High Domino Tipping Match

RAVEN HIT US from above – diving down from out of the clouds and making a loud and dangerous thump on the top of the big pink Winnebago that sounded a little like a kettle drum beating up on a peal of rolling thunder in the middle of a twenty-one gun salute.

"Holy old baldheaded moose stink," Bigfoot bellowed. "What's raining down on the tin roof privy now?"

"HANG ON TO YOUR TOOTSIE ROLLS!" the Prophet yelled. "WE'RE GONNA ROLL OUT OF CONTROL!"

Which is exactly what happened – we rolled out of control - the pink Winnebago nearly turning over in mid-air, rolling sideways like a great pink man-eating whale shark, drunk and dizzy on way too much tabasco sauce.

I fell over into a sort of a slow-motion somersault across the back of Coyote who was busy struggling with the Warren-cocoon which had slid across the floor of the pink Winnebago and had slammed into Coyote's stomach.

Why don't you try saying that five times fast?

KA-BANG!

Raven hit us again, this time even harder.

I never dreamed that a stupid bird could be that strong. I mean what was a bird, really? Nothing but wings and feathers and whole lot of squawk – but who would have thought a bird could hit like this one could.

"That Raven is beginning to irritate me," Bigfoot growled. "I've got to get out of here and get my hands on that Raven and instruct him in the fine art of chicken plucking. Somebody better take this wheel from me now."

Only I was way too busy trying to hang onto Warren.

"Don't let go of my steering wheel!" the Prophet yelled back. "We will fall like a fast-frozen rock if I don't have anyone steering."

BOOM!

"We're going to fall anyway!" Bigfoot yelled.

The big pink Winnebago tilted and the Warren-cocoon slid towards the door – which had swung open and was hanging from its bright pink hinges.

"Bow-woo! Bow-woo! Bow-woo!"

I could see Old Shuck standing in the middle of the Gulf of St. Lawrence on top of the back of a less-than-happy humpback whale barking in sheer frustrated desperation. From all the way this far up Old Shuck looked like a tiny little grape Chihuahua but his bark carried just fine. I guess he wanted to get at that Raven nearly as badly as Bigfoot did – but both Bigfoot and Old Shuck were way too far away to help me much.

I caught a glimpse of Raven as he flew by the flapping Winnebago door.

He was having himself a fine old time - laughing like he had inhaled about thirty-eight tanks full of pure undiluted giggle gas. I guess he thought we looked pretty funny – spinning out of control the way we were.

"SOMEBODY DO SOMETHING!" Bigfoot yelled at no one in particular.

BOOM-BA-BOOM!

Raven hit us one more time again.

The Warren-cocoon bounced a little and began to roll a little bit more – steadily moving towards the open Winnebago door. I made a sort of a clumsy leap for it and reached my hands out just far enough and hard enough to sink my fingers into the skin of the Warren-cocoon.

I could feel Warren's life-force pulsing into my fingertips. I wasn't sure if I was soaking him up or if he was soaking me up. I could feel something that was yellow and blue and green and tasted like a cold rusted penny and I might have even peed my pants a little and I knew that I was more scared than I had ever been in my lifetime but I hung onto the Warren-cocoon like it was the last thing that I would ever do.

And then I heard Warren talking to me – like he was talking in another room a thousand miles away over a very bad telephone connection.

"It will be okay, Adam,' the voice of Warren said. "Just you wait and see."

I didn't have all that long to wait.

BOOM-BALOOM!

Raven hit us again.

The Warren-cocoon bounced even harder and then it slid right out the door with me still hanging onto it. I stuck one foot out against the left side of the doorway and the other foot against the right side and I hung on for dear life – barely managing to hold onto the Warren-cocoon.

I could see Warren and I could see my Dad and the two faces were flashing in front of me like a playing card clothes-pinned onto a spinning bicycle wheel.

And then Coyote was standing directly beside me – with his teeth sunk down into my left leg – trying to haul me back inside.

I could feel his teeth digging in and even though I knew that he was doing his best not to hurt me much – he was also doing his level best to hang onto my leg – which meant he had to bite down hard.

Which hurt.

A whole lot.

"OWWW!" I yelled.

"Stmmmm Cmphlighning," Coyote mumbled – which I think was him asking me to stop complaining – only my leg kept getting in the way of proper enunciation.

And then he bit down harder.

"Owww!" I yelled, nearly as loud as Bigfoot.

And then I kicked Coyote with my other leg.

It wasn't that hard of a kick and I didn't really mean to do it. It was just sort of instinctive. It was just as instinctive a move as him biting down on my leg even harder in return.

"Owww!!!" I howled out – twice as loud as Bigfoot had EVER yelled.

And I kicked again – only this time Coyote yanked his head backwards – pulling me and the Warren-cocoon back into the safety of The Prophet.

Great, I thought. We're winning.

And then Raven grabbed hold of the far end of the Warren-cocoon.

Great, I thought. Now we're NOT winning nearly as much as we had been.

I could see the Godzilla-sized bird somehow reaching in and shrinking down just enough to catch hold of the end of the Warren-cocoon with his beak. I had never seen so big a bird from this close up before now but I'm pretty sure that Raven was grinning at me.

"I'm losing him," I shouted – meaning the Warren-cocoon. "Pull harder."

"UMPH-LOOGHEN-HUM," Coyote mouthed over my leg – meaning that he was losing his grip on me.

The whole time Raven kept on laughing. I guess that he had never seen anything half as funny as the two of us jammed up together on top of each other in that mystic pink motor home doorway, hanging onto that big fuzzy Warren-cocoon with all of our might.

Did you ever watch a domino tipping match? You know – where somebody with a WHOLE lot of spare time on their hands will lay out some really cool sort of a design – like maybe a maple leaf or a map of the Yukon Territories or the outline of a fully grown bull moose just by lining up a giant forever-long row of dominos?

And THEN – once they have got that entire moose/maple-leaf/map=of-the-Yukon laid out then they'll crouch down and give that very first domino just a tiny little flick just hard enough to tip that next domino which tips into the third domino and finally that entire moose or maple leaf or Yukon Territory map is nothing more than a long mess of dominoes laying on the floor waiting for somebody to pick them back up.

Well that was just sort of how it went with me and Coyote and the Warren-cocoon and Raven. We were stuck at what my geeky chess-playing step-dad Warren – whom I was clinging onto for dear sweet life – would have called a stalemate.

Until Bigfoot jumped in.

<u>Chapter Twenty Six – Raven, Prepare to be Plucked</u>

IT HAPPENED LIKE this.

First I heard The Prophet asking somebody that I couldn't exactly see just what the heck they thought they were doing.

No, I don't know why The Prophet said that.

Like I said I just heard it, is all.

Then the next thing I heard was Bigfoot replying loudly that he was going to do something – so I guess maybe it was Bigfoot that The Prophet had been talking to in the first place.

And then Bigfoot did something.

In spades.

Only I still didn't see a thing that was happening around me.

That's just how it goes, isn't it? Most things that affect you in this life go on without you ever really seeing how it went.

Your Mom falls out of love with your very own Dad and then decides that a divorce is a really good idea.

You didn't see that happen.

Your Dad gets blown up by a baby carriage full of roofing nails.

You didn't see that happen either.

That's how life works.

All you ever have to live on and follow are stories that other people tell you. The important things in life are USUALLY the things that you can't feel or touch – or even see.

So I DIDN'T see Bigfoot letting go of The Prophet's steering wheel.

And I DIDN'T see Bigfoot leaping in my direction.

"Where are you going?" the Prophet asked again in a panic sounding voice – which didn't do much for my confidence at all.

"To do something," I heard Bigfoot replying. "I could use a little help if you could spare it."

And then all at once Bigfoot let go of the wheel and stood behind me and caught hold of both of my shoulders and then he jammed both of his feet squarely against the wall of the Winnebago – and me and Coyote and Bigfoot must have looked like a three-man bobsled team trying to luge down four hundred feet invisible ski trail in the sky.

"Here we go," the Prophet yelled. "Bottom floor, coming up."

The big pink mystical motor home veered wildly out of control – with no one at the steering wheel. The Prophet was still beating his wings but it was like watching your drunken uncle trying to learn how to polka dance after the band had stopped playing. He couldn't seem to fly in a straight line at all.

We hurtled downwards like a giant pink comet.

I could see the Labrador shoreline just ahead of us but I wasn't certain if we were going to land on the shore or the ocean or maybe just crash and burn and die.

That was a really cheerful thought, wasn't it?

The very last thing I remember was the feeling of Warren slipping away as the Raven pulled him free from my grip – and the taste of salty choked-back tears funneling down my screaming throat while Bigfoot pulled me back into the safety of the giant pink mystical travel home that was busily falling out of the sky.

"Hang on," Bigfoot told me – only he did not give me a single clue as to exactly WHAT I ought to be hanging on to.

Then he pulled me up and then he even managed to grab hold of Warren and pull him up too – and I can still see that look of consternation and disgust on the beak of that Raven after Bigfoot had yanked my cocoon-stepdad out from his grasp - and then all at once Bigfoot let go of my hands, kicked off straight out the side door of The Prophet and launched himself directly at the onlooking Raven.

"GEE-RON-AH-MO-BANZAI!" Bigfoot yelled.

I had to grin at that war whoop of Bigfoot as he entered freefall.

That reckless yell meant one thing and one thing only.

Raven feathers were going to be plucked

I would have sat back and enjoyed the show – but I was WAY too busy trying my best to hang onto my stepdad and to not to fall out of the giant pink drunken-uncle-polka-dancing Winnebago and down to my death below.

It's important to remember that.

A fellow has GOT to keep his priorities straight.

Chapter Twenty Seven – A Giant Geronimo Free Fall Pancake

I'VE GOT TO admit that Bigfoot almost looked weirdly pretty and maybe even just a little bit graceful hung out there in thin mid-air with his arms spread wide like a giant furry sky-diving wanna-be-paratrooper Wookie.

Mind you, I am not really sure just what Bigfoot was actually thinking, jumping out of the safety of The Prophet like that.

I mean, Raven had a whole lot more options when it came to aerial maneuverability.

Raven could turn to the left or the right. He could fly straight up or he could spiral downwards or he could just flap his wings and hover there for a little while.

As a bird – when it came to sky – Raven had a whole lot of possible options.

Bigfoot – on the other hand – had one single undeniable choice, and that one choice was to fall straight down - which is why it kind of surprised me when Raven banked and turned in such a way as to meet Bigfoot in a perfect mid-air collision.

Which was about the time that The Prophet tilted and spun and I almost lost my grip upon the slippery goop of the Warren-cocoon one more time – which almost slid and fell out of the side door of the mystic pink Winnebago, yet again.

Sometimes it seems as if life is nothing more than a whole lot of doing the same thing over and over and over again until something finally works.

"DAD!" I shouted, nearly jumping out of the Winnebago myself.

Yeah, I know.

I went and I said the "D-word", directly in Warren's direction.

It didn't matter that Warren hadn't actually heard me yelling that "D-word" – what with him being covered by that mystical pine needle cocoon of his.

It was still the "D-word".

Meaning, Dad.

And I had said it at Warren.

I almost jumped, too. I don't really know what I thought I could accomplish by jumping but I still felt that knee-jerk of reflex galvanizing through the calves of my legs and the only thing that stopped me from hurtling out of that door towards certain death was Coyote hanging onto me for dear sweet life.

Raven kept on coming towards Bigfoot and Bigfoot was primed and ready.

I watched as Bigfoot grabbed a fistful of midnight black feathers with his big left hand as he hurtled past Raven, bringing his big right fist hooking upwards into a wonderfully beautiful right hook.

"POW!!!" Bigfoot yelled – just as his right fist hit home.

I'm not really sure if yelling pow made him hit any harder – but Raven shook the right hook off and handed Bigfoot a hook of his own – namely he drove that giant heavy beak of his deep down into Bigfoot's shoulder meat.

I saw something red spilling down Bigfoot's shoulder – and it didn't look like ketchup to me at all.

"OW!!!" Bigfoot yelled.

Meanwhile, the Warren-cocoon slipped a little further out the door and the Prophet kept on falling and the Labrador dirt was coming up fast.

"Do something!" I shouted – not sure if I was talking to Coyote, the Prophet, to Warren, or even possibly to myself.

Gravity is funny, that way. It works awfully quick, whenever you don't want it to.

"I am falling just as fast as I can," the Prophet yelled back. "Maybe if I am careful I can land on top of Bigfoot and break my fall – once the Raven decides to let go of him."

At the same time Raven ripped upwards with his heavy talons, slashing and tearing deep vicious gouges out of Bigfoot's big furry belly. I saw more red not-ketchup spilling out of Bigfoot's belly-fur.

Bigfoot didn't seem to be bothered by that not-ketchup. He took another solid swing – only this punch had about half as much of the "POW!!!" of his first swing.

"Pow!" Bigfoot weakly yelled.

Maybe he should have yelled just a little bit louder – because Raven easily dodged Bigfoot's second punch. Raven banked to the left, shaking his head so that Bigfoot swung like the world's largest and fuzziest set of dog tags you had ever seen - and then Raven twisted his head down and caught hold of one of the feathers that Bigfoot was hanging onto.

At which point Raven pulled that vital feather loose and then he reached down and yanked out another of the feathers that Bigfoot was hanging onto.

This feather-yanking didn't seem to be hurting Raven one bit – any more than it would hurt you or me to pluck a hair out of our head – but it was making it awfully hard for Bigfoot to hang on. Each feather yanked meant one less feather for him to hang onto - and then he dropped.

Meanwhile the Labrador landscape was getting a whole lot closer.

By now it was becoming a bit of a guessing-match as to which of us was going to hit first.

The Warren-cocoon, Bigfoot or the Prophet.

With us inside.

"Hang on, Adam," Coyote gravel-whispered in my ear. "Think about feathers in a soft summer updraft."

I felt myself being wrapped up in a gray fuzzy crash blanket as Coyote wrapped himself entirely about me and the Warren-cocoon and then we jumped out of The Prophet's door.

It was a cool and wonderful kind of experience. I'm not quite sure how he did it. According to every rule of gravity that existed we should have been falling at the exact same rate of speed that the Prophet had been falling at the time that Coyote had jumped.

Only we didn't fall.

It felt as if Coyote was made out of nothing but dandelion dandruff and dust motes. We sort of hovered – not really flying – just lofting a little upwards and then sort of floating gently down to the dirt. I could see out of the corner of my eye Coyote's big pink tongue lolling happily in the breeze all the while him grinning a big old happy Coyote grin.

I guess he was feeling pretty pleased with himself - which was right about when I noticed that Coyote had those two freshly-plucked Raven feathers sticking out of his big Coyote grin. I don't know how he managed to catch those feathers and if Bigfoot had actually MEANT to drift them Coyote's way, but Coyote was sure feeling pretty happy and more than a little bit smug about catching those magic Raven feathers and using them to float the way that he did.

And I guess I couldn't blame him one little bit.

We landed as if we had been falling through water. I almost felt as if someone were filming me in slow motion – like I was falling in some kind of a dream space.

Just try and think about feathers, he had said – and that's exactly what I was trying hard to think about.

I was thinking about feathers and I was thinking about freshly-blown soap bubbles on a hot summer evening and I was thinking about moon-walking astronauts, dandelion fluff and bright billowy cotton candy parachutes.

And whether it was my soft-headed thinking or Raven's magic feathers or just plain dumb luck we landed and we stood there in the Labrador dirt and watched as Bigfoot and the Prophet crashed to the ground like a giant Geronimo free fall pancake.

I'm not saying it was pretty.

"WE'VE GOT TO SAVE HIM!" I screamed. "HE'S GOING TO FREAKING CRASH AND DIE!"

"I'm open for any sort of suggestions you can think of," Coyote said. "But as far as I can see we are REALLY short on options."

I reached down and I laid my hand upon the Warren-cocoon and I could feel a sort of warm comforting tingle as if someone were reaching up through the pine and swamp grass sides of the big funky sticky cocoon and holding onto my hand saying there, there, everything is going to be all right.

Namely, Warren.

And then all at once I saw The Prophet soaring down in a sort of semi-controlled crash dive. He seemed to be almost aiming himself towards the plummeting Bigfoot.

Bigfoot kept on falling.

The Prophet moved a little closer.

The ground came closer too.

And then all of a sudden everything got WAY too close.

Chapter Twenty Eight – Dead and Back Again

THE WAY IT happened was like this.

The Prophet waited until he was just close enough and then he opened up a hatch in his side that hadn't been there before. I guess that he was figuring on catching Bigfoot with that hatch door and scooping him up like a big pink Tonka bulldozer. Only his timing was just that much off and instead of scooping Bigfoot up that freshly-opened hatch caught the big hairy Sasquatch in the side of his ribs and Bigfoot took a triple and a half flying Lutz-Eagle over the top of the hatch door and then fell the rest of the way straight down to the ground.

It might have broken his fall just a little but it might also have broken his ribcage.

I'm NOT saying it was pretty.

"Oops," Coyote said. "Nice try."

It WAS an awfully good try.

Too bad it did not work.

"This is going to hurt him a whole lot more than it hurts me," Coyote said, squinting – but not looking away.

Bigfoot hit the ground awfully hard.

Do you want to know how hard he hit?

Just try and imagine what it would look like if King Kong had dropped a slightly-used Barbie Doll with a dog-sized-rock chained securely around her tiny pink plastic ankles from about a thousand feet higher than the tip-top of the Empire State Building.

Just try to imagine the sort of impact that the plastic vinyl of that dog-chained Barbie Doll might make, falling from that far up.

Then multiply that impact by a couple of dozen infinities.

Bigfoot hit that hard – and then some.

I saw the dirt around him kind of sink in – like a heavy boot sinking into a deep spring mud puddle.

Oh good – I thought – the dirt was soft and it absorbed his impact and he is safe and alive and everything is going to be okay.

Yeah, right.

My golly, but what a great big fat bunch of lies we can tell ourselves in about three and a half seconds worth of thinking.

I took off running to the crash site.

Coyote was running close behind me.

When I got there Bigfoot was lying quietly in a patch of tall grass. His face was the approximate color of sunburned rust and there was all of that not-ketchup and he had more bruises than the world's rottenest apple and as far as I could tell he was just barely breathing.

"Is he dead?" I asked Coyote. "He can't be dead."

Nothing.

"He can't be dead," I repeated. "He's practically mythical."

I said that last word loudly – hoping that Bigfoot would open his eyes and look up at me and maybe dryly say something about how I must be three hundred and eighteen kinds of stupid for even daring to call him mythical – only he didn't budge.

He did not say anything at all.

I didn't know what to think. I was struck dumb and stupid, all at once - and then Bigfoot groaned softly.

It was one of the most wonderful sounds I had ever heard.

"I knew it," I said. "Bigfoots can't die."

"Not hardly," Bigfoot weakly mumbled. "Not yet, anyway."

He still didn't sound very healthy but I was grasping at straws and happy at the feel of hay between my fingertips.

"I just KNEW it." I said. "I knew that you couldn't be dead."

I know just how absolutely gorky that sounded – but remember – I had just skydived about two billion light years out of a pink mystical Winnebago – wrapped in the raven-feathered skin of a mystical trickster Coyote.

Things like that will wear on a fellow.

"Of course I'm not dead," Bigfoot said. "Stories never die. They're just retold in a different kind of a way."

It was at that point that The Prophet crashed down into the Labrador terrain at a speed of about a billion miles a minute.

Now let me tell you - Labrador is a very rough piece of territory.

It is just about the size of the state of Nevada – or slightly bigger than the nation of Japan – and over twice as large as the entire United Kingdom – covering over one hundred and fifty thousand square miles of thinly soiled rocky terrain.

It is a country of green and gray and white. Green in the summer, fat and full of boreal forests, peaty swamps and sprawling lush meadow land – but in the winter the whole thing ices up and the entire landscape snoozes beneath a blanket of thick white snow.

"Green or white," Bigfoot had told me earlier. "You just can't escape the grey of the underlying rock structure. There are more geological deposits in this patch of landscape than you could shake a truckload of nuclear geologists at."

That is a whole lot of rock.

The big mystical pink Winnebago had crashed down upon the long curving ridge of a glacial esker – which is what my geography teacher would have called that long winding snake-like ridge of granite and glacially-paved gravel.

The sides of the mystic Winnebago crushed in as it impacted upon that hard unyielding granite. The windows shattered and I heard the Prophet screaming in agony. One of the wheel tires had flown off like the world's ugliest UFO. I saw that wheel tire Frisbee-ing across the skyline to smash into the branches of a stunted cedar.

I could hear the sound of children yelling stories.

I could hear the crackle of pages being turned and crumpled and thrown into a barrel of burning oil.

I could hear the firecracker rattle of electrons and ions working together – and could hear the sound of my stepdad Warren telling me one more story - but there were no flames.

The Prophet was a mystical travel home and did not require gasoline – but that did not make the impact and destruction any less terrifying to see this close up.

"We've got company," Coyote said.

I turned back around just in time to see an army of tiny gray figures rising up out of the tall yellowed Labrador grass.

The figures were tiny and ugly and they were all carrying very nasty looking spears. They had formed a protective circle about Bigfoot's big body. I wasn't sure if they were guarding him or if they were just trying to keep me and Coyote away from him.

Bigfoot groaned again.

"Now we're in for it," Coyote said. "This is not good."

I wanted to run and charge right through those mean-looking tiny men – spears or not – but Coyote grabbed me by the shoulder and held me back.

"Mannegishi," Coyote said to the little men, holding his paw-hands out to show he meant no harm. "We come in peace."

Peaceful or not, the Mannegishi – whatever that meant – did not seem to be in the mood for any sort of an amicable negotiation.

The tallest of the Mannegishi – who was maybe about four feet tall and twice as skinny – gestured with his spear and Coyote started walking in the direction that the Mannegishi intended him to go.

As for me I just kept staring back at the wreckage of the Winnebago.

I saw a heavy black rain cloud in the distance, sort of drifting through the otherwise bright blue sky.

It was kind of funny. I had seen a rain cloud the very first time I met The Prophet. He'd been hiding inside of it – but as far as I could tell that cloud I was looking at now wasn't anything more than a plain old rain cloud and all that it most likely signified was that we were most likely going to get wet fairly soon.

That is, if we ACTUALLY survived the Mannegishi – not to mention the Raven.

Still, I could not escape the feeling that the rain cloud was actually trying to tell me something in some kind of secret smoke-signal cloud language.

I expect that the only real story that cloud was trying to tell me was "You might want to think about buying yourself an umbrella and a big old raincoat" – but to me that little black cloud looked a little bit too much like a raven in flight.

I didn't care.

Not one bit at all.

The Prophet was dead.

Bigfoot was almost dead.

Warren was most likely dead.

My Dad was definitely dead.

It all boiled down to one single undeniable truth.

The Raven had won.

How bad could things get from where they were at?

I felt like I was in the middle of one of those forever-long nightmares that you sometimes get – those ones in which you are falling and every time it seems that you are going to hit the bottom a trapdoor opens and you keep on falling.

But I was pretty sure that I had hit rock bottom, two or three trapdoors ago.

In fact, right about now I figured I would have to look straight up past the crow cloud to even see rock bottom – and I might even need a couple of Hubbell Space Telescopes to see it with.

And then – at that point in which I figured that I could no longer fall any further than I had - something worse happened.

A figure stepped up from behind a hill.

It was a man.

I could not see his face from this far away.

I watched the unknown man walking towards me with that slow and steady lope as if he had walking towards me for all of his life.

Something about the way that he walked looked awfully scarily familiar to me.

"Hi Adam," the figure said to me. "It has been a very long time since we both really got the chance to talk."

I knew that voice.

I opened my mouth.

Then I closed my mouth back up again.

So far as I could tell no words fell out between that opening and closing.

"It's good to see you again," the figure said. "Aren't you even going to say hello?"

Open.

Close.

One more time.

Still nothing falling out.

"You don't have anything to say to me at all?" the figure asked me.

It was my Dad, of course.

My real Dad.

Dead – and back again.

I guess it's true what Coyote told me.

I guess, deep down, that I always knew it was as true as true could ever grow.

Stories never die.

Chapter Twenty Nine – All of the Peanut Butter Sandwiches in the World

SO JUST THINK on how this would hit you – if you were me and I was somebody else sitting at home watching an Arnold Schwarzenegger movie while you were going through all of this commotion. You have to understand that all I REALLY had to go on was mostly the stories that my Mother had sort of told me along the way and PARTLY the stories that she didn't ever get around to telling me and I guess maybe I made up the rest of it from a few old photographs and a couple of half-remembered memories that might have been nothing more than daydreams and a bit of wishful thinking.

I had fully believed that my Dad was dead – killed outside of a little Afghanistan village by a homemade exploding baby carriage.

Heck, I had even watched the whole thing happen – thanks to the dream vision freak-out that the Raven and the Sleeping Giant had sent me on.

And now here he was walking towards me just as big as life – my very own Dad - now standing there and staring at me and smiling that half-crooked grin of his that I remembered from all of those pictures that my Mom had shown me.

"Dad?" I said.

I knew it had to be some kind of a trick – but the part of me that had never ever wanted to let go of this man's memory just didn't want to let go of the crazy impossible notion that he might actually still be alive.

"Why don't you hush up now, would you?" my real Dad said, pointing directly at Coyote – who promptly closed his mouth tight. In fact, if Coyote's mouth had been an open door it had just got slammed shut, all by itself.

I looked at Coyote in disbelief.

He just stood there, those two raven feathers still sticking out of his mouth with a look of perpetual stupid frozen upon his big fuzzy dog-like features. He might as well have been stuffed with sawdust for all of the talking that he was suddenly not doing.

I didn't think that ANYTHING would shut him up.

"Hi, Adam," my real Dad said to me, holding his arms open wide for a hug. "How about a hug for the old man?"

A part of me wanted to run just about as fast as my feet could carry me and throw myself directly into that wide open hug he was offering me - but another part of me – the part that was thinking how much that hug looked like a freshly-set bear trap – wanted to run twice as fast in the other direction.

"You're dead," I said. "Aren't you?"

Dad just laughed and shook his head in a kind of a television-dad style – like he had been rehearsing that head-shake in front of the bathroom mirror all week long.

No, this wasn't my Dad.

This was not my Dad at all.

It could not be.

"Do I look dead?" he asked me.

I looked at Bigfoot.

He was still moaning a little.

He looked dead.

"What about my friend?" I asked, pointing at Bigfoot.

"The Mannegishi will take care of him," the thing that looked like my Dad said. "You don't have to worry about anything at all."

And then he said something to the Mannegishi in that language of theirs that sounded a little bit like the cawing of crows, wind moving through the autumn-dead leaves and about fifty-eight thousand empty pop bottles crashing onto a shout of frozen concrete.

"That's fine," Coyote said.

And then my Dad pointed at Coyote.

"They'll take care of him too."

"That's just fine," Coyote repeated in a voice as flat as a steam-rollered shadow.

I saw at least a dozen of the Mannegishi spread out and surround Coyote. There was more of that crow-caw glass-shouting.

"I sure wish I knew what they were saying," I said out loud. "I'd feel a whole lot more comfortable about what is going on."

"Oh I can fix that," Dad said.

Then he caught me by both of my shoulders and looked me straight in the eye like he was about to have a long and intense conversation with me about something that I did not want to talk about. Then he opened up his mouth and words began to fall out like a sudden summer downpour. It was almost like he was speed-shouting into my brain. I could see his mouth moving only it was like a movie where someone had sped the camera up and I saw flashes of understanding going off inside of me like the rattle of fireworks and then all a sudden I knew how to speak Mannegishi.

It was that fast.

All at once I could understand the crow-cawing bottle-breaking words of the Mannegishi and I kind of had the feeling that they were laughing and joking at me and Bigfoot and Coyote – like a group of schoolyard bullies getting set to play one of the meanest tricks in high school history on some poor misguided dweeb.

Namely, me.

"Your mother never really told you all that much about me did she?" Dad asked.

"I thought she had told me nearly everything there was to know," I replied. I wasn't sure if I was talking in English or Mannegishi or both at the same time – but Dad seemed to understand me all right as he crooked about one-third of a grin in my direction – like he was saving some of it back for later on.

"Not hardly," he said. "Not by a long old shot – but I will definitely tell you about it in just a little while."

That wasn't good enough for me.

"Why not just tell it to me now?" I asked.

"Now THAT is a story that will take some sneaking up on," Dad explained. "I'm not nearly half as good at the telling of things as some people are."

Do you know that I would swear that he was staring straight at the Warren-cocoon when he said that? Besides - I still wasn't satisfied that everything had been properly taken care of. I looked over at the wreckage of what used to be The Prophet.

"What about him?" I asked, nodding at The Prophet.

I was more than a little surprised to realize that I was speaking in Mannegishi when I said that and I guess my surprise must have tickled some of the Mannegishi warriors because it brought on another onslaught of laughing and giggling.

"They're laughing at your terrible accent," Dad said. "The way you speak Mannegishi - I have to admit, it is pretty funny."

I have an accent?

"But what about HIM?" I repeated, raising my voice and trying to correct my accent – although I wasn't sure what was wrong with it in the first place.

Dad's eyes went wide and he sort of half-smiled at my question like he thought I was kidding him or something.

"Him? You mean the Winnebago?" Dad asked. "Son, that vehicle has been totaled. Even you have got to see that. There are just some things that aren't worth saving. We'll just have to walk from here on out – unless you happen to have a pet Smart Car hidden somewhere in your Batman backpack."

My friend – The Prophet - was dead.

Dad said it like someone might tell you that you had just lost a dime through a hole in your pocket.

He said it like it wasn't all that big of a deal.

He said it like he didn't really care.

"But that's my friend," I said.

This time Dad laughed right out loud and that one-third of a grin snapped open like a sprung switchblade.

"So your best friend is a big pink motor home?" Dad said. "Do you get a lot of mileage out of that relationship?"

Oh yes, I supposed you have noticed that I had begun using the "D-word" again.

See – as many as times as I kept saying to myself that this guy WAS my Dad or this guy WASN'T my Dad my mind kept on flip-flopping like a Band-Aid that would not stay stuck down fast.

"And don't forget Warren," I said. "Is he going to be okay too?"

"Warren who?" Dad asked.

Okay.

So now what do I say?

Do I tell this guy who looks so much like what I imagine my real Dad would look like that the Mom that he might actually have married had went and married another man while he was dead in Afghanistan – or maybe not dead?

Dead Dad.

Dad not Dead.

You are dead. You are not my Dad anymore. Some other dude is now my stepdad.

Only he might be dead too.

It was getting awfully confusing for me. There were WAY too many D-words going on in this whole conversation for my liking.

"I don't know what to tell you," was all I could come up with.

"It'll most likely come to you," Dad replied.

I nodded like I wasn't exactly sure of what he was telling me.

"Look," Dead-Dad said to me. "There's not much we can do right now – standing here in the middle of this wilderness. Why don't you come home with me?"

"To Afghanistan?" I asked.

I know how stupid that sounded – but you try and come up with something sensible to say the next time that YOUR Dad comes back from the dead.

Dad just shook his head and smiled the very same smile that he had smiled from off of the photograph on the fireplace mantle back home.

"No," Dad said. "Not Afghanistan. I live right here in the woods of Labrador. And don't ask me why. There is WAY too much to explain right now. Just understand that I've been living with the Mannegishi for a very long time now and you can come and stay at my place and once we've had a good solid meal I'll explain the whole story to you."

Great.

Just what I needed.

One more story.

"Is that okay with you son?"

Hearing that last word said by the only man that I ever wanted to hear it from was all that I really needed to change my mind.

"Sure Dad," I said.

And then I hugged him.

Whether it was a dream, a story or an outright lie – I wasn't going to miss this opportunity - not for all of the peanut butter sandwiches and Kool-Aid in the whole wide world.

I was that happy.

"I can't believe what I'm seeing," I said. "Dad, I've got so many things to tell you."

Which was right about when Old Shuck galloped up from out of the woods. He took one look at my Dad – and that big purple Death Dog began to growl.

Loudly.

Chapter Thirty – You Better Quit Kicking My Dog Around

OLD SHUCK CONTINUED to growl.

GRRRRRRRRR...

I could see one thing very clearly.

Old Shuck did NOT like this new Dad – not one single bit.

"Is that your dog?" back-from-the-dead Dad asked me.

GRRRRRRRRR...

"He's my friend," I said, just a little bit too defensively. "I wouldn't exactly call him my dog. He just walks with me, is all."

GRRRRRRRRRRR...

"Well you ought to teach your friend better manners," Dad said. "In fact, I don't think that I really care all that much at all for your dog-friend's company."

I put my hand on Old Shuck's neck, just hard enough to hold him back just a little – although of course, if that big old purple Death Dog had REALLY wanted to move I couldn't hold him back any more than a twelve year old Girl Scout could hold back a freshly-cut full-sized redwood tree from timbering on down.

Come to think of it the Girl Scout would probably stand a better chance.

"Go on, Shuck," I told him. "Go on over there with Coyote. I'll be all right over here by himself. I'm just talking to my Dad, is all."

Wasn't I?

Old Shuck growled a little bit more but he listened to what I had told him. He walked slowly over to stand directly beside Coyote – who was still standing there with that goofy look on his face and those two goofy Raven feathers sticking out of his mouth like he had been caught eating an unplucked chicken dinner.

And all the time Old Shuck kept on growling at Dad-not-Dad.

GRRRRRRRRRRRRRRRRRR…

I stood there beside my Dad.

Not-Dad.

Did you ever hear that little voice that whispers to you sometimes whenever you are getting set to do something that you REALLY ought not to do?

Well, that was the voice.

"Dad," I said – trying hard to drown that quiet little voice out. "It is SO good to see you."

Oddly enough, I almost meant what I was saying – in spite of that little voice that kept on whispering *not-dad* to me. I mean – I had already pretty well lost Warren and Bigfoot and The Prophet. Who could really blame me for not wanting to lose anyone else?

"A dog like that REALLY ought to be tied up," Dad-not-Dad said. "You do know that, now don't you?"

Then Dad-not-Dad looked at me and he smiled like he was thinking about a bottle of cold grape soda pop that he had left in the refrigerator back home just waiting for after he had got done walking home from Afghanistan on a long hot summer day.

"Speaking of tying," Dad-not-Dad said – right before he reached over and tied two black raven feathers in my hair. He did it fast – like he had been tying feathers into people's hair for about as long as birds grew wings. He braided each of those feathers up in about as much time as it took you to read this sentence.

It was that fast.

And all at once I felt a deep calm wash over me – like when your Mom tucks a blanket up around your chin and tells you that it is time for you to go to sleep and dream about a world where teachers hand you out A-filled report cards just because you stayed at home all day watching cartoons on your television set.

"That's fine," I said.

"Fine," Coyote echoed.

And then Dad-not-Dad looked back at Old Shuck – who was still growling in Dad-not-Dad's general direction.

"Yes sir," Dad-not-Dad said. "A dog like that just REALLY ought to be tied up."

Then he nodded and before I knew it a couple of dozen of those tiny Mannegishi had begun to circle around Old Shuck, carrying lassoes.

"That's fine," I said.

"Just fine," Coyote echoed.

It was funny.

A part of me was wondering just WHY my Dad-not-Dad was so darned determined to tie up Old Shuck – but heck – maybe he just didn't like dogs, is all. Which was really kind of surprising. I mean, that was something that I never knew about my Dad-not-Dad but there is an awful lot of things that a kid like me doesn't know about a Dad who went and died and came back from the dead just like my Dad just did.

Not-Dad.

Of course, trying to throw a rope around Old Shuck was an awful lot of wasted energy. Even I could have told them if they had thought to ask me about it. The first three lassoes fell directly onto Old Shuck's neck and he took off like a dream of running wind with those three Mannegishi warriors just hanging on for pure sweet life. Two of the Mannegishi thought to let go but the third warrior must have had his hand snagged or else he was just too scare or too stupid to let go. Either way, Old Shuck took off into the Labrador wilderness like he was fixing to run half past forever – with that third stupid warrior bouncing behind him in the dirt like a drunken lead-plated kite's tail.

Darn it.

That was most likely the very last that I was going to see of Old Shuck – which bothered me a lot because I had actually begun to LIKE that big smelly purple old death dog – but then I felt that deep black calm wash over me.

Who cares – I thought.

Who cares about an old purple dog just so long as I have got my Dad with me again.

Not-Dad.

Dad.

Not-Dad.

Dad.

"Good riddance," Dad-not-Dad said. "I hope that mangy animal keeps on running until he hits the ocean and drowns."

"That's fine," I said – wondering to myself just exactly why had it taken me so very long to discover just how truly fine the word "fine" felt like when you kept on saying it.

I mean, just try saying it, right now.

Fine.

You just can't help but smile when you say that word out loud.

Fine.

"Just fine," Coyote echoed.

"You still talk too much," Dad-not-Dad said to Coyote. "But I can fix that."

Then Dad walked over to where Coyote was standing. I saw him pull a long thin bone needle out from shirt, as well as a spool of dirty white cord. Then, before you could say Singer sewing machine my Dad stitched a long nasty running stitch across Coyote's mouth.

"Now that's fine," Dad-not-Dad said, with a grin that wasn't anywhere close to a happy grin.

"Jph fhn," Coyote mumbled through the stitches in reply.

And then my Dad looked over at Bigfoot.

I didn't actually like the way that Dad-not-Dad was looking at Bigfoot but the feathers kept on telling me never you mind.

"All right," Dad-not-Dad said to the crowd of Mannegishi, pointing down at what was left of Bigfoot. "Take care of him!"

The Mannegishi raised their long sharp spears high over their heads.

They paused for just a minute, like they were waiting for some kind of an alarm to go off or else maybe some sort of cosmic omen.

I knew what they were going to do.

You would have to be ten kinds of stupid not to see it coming.

But I just stood there and smiled calmly - and then they drove those long sharp spears down – directly into what was left of Bigfoot's big hairy chest.

"That's fine," I said.

Chapter Thirty One – Taking Care of Bigfoot

THE MANNEGISHI RAISED their spears up, pulling them up forcibly out from what was left of Bigfoot.

I could see the dark red chili-con-carne Bigfoot blood dripping down from off of the ends of all of those long sharp nasty-looking spears. I could feel a part of myself screaming way down deep inside of the sub-sub-sub-basement of my being – but at the very same time I felt a flat cellophane smile plaster itself over my mouth as the Mannegishi drove their spears a second time down into Bigfoot's chest.

Again and again and again.

"That's just fine," I said – still smiling as calm as a saucer of warm milk on the outside of me but deep down inside I was screaming just as loudly as I could imagine.

Not Dad.

Dad-not-Dad walked over to Bigfoot's body.

He was grinning while he was walking.

It wasn't a very nice grin at all.

"You thought you were too big for me, didn't you?" Dad-not-Dad said.

Then Dad-not-Dad sat down in the dirt behind Bigfoot's fallen body.

"You thought that you were such big shot with all of your newspaper stories and television shows, didn't you?" Dad-not-Dad went on. "You always thought that you were the only story that was going to never ever die."

I stood there and watched calmly as Dad-not-Dad planted both of his feet squarely upon Bigfoot's shoulder blades.

For a moment I thought of the way that Bigfoot had planted both of his big hairy feet before he had pulled me back into The Prophet when we were falling out of the sky – maybe ten minutes and a hundred million years ago.

I kept on watching as Dad-not-Dad carefully wrapped his hands beneath Bigfoot's big hairy chin and ears.

"You thought you were better than any of us."

I watched as Dad-not-Dad dug his fingers as deeply as he could into Bigfoot's neck. I watched as he grunted and strained -, the muscles in his back flexing like a pair of huge wings - until he yanked Bigfoot's head off of his shoulders like some spoiled little kid might yank the head of an unsuspecting action figure.

It should not have happened.

There wasn't any way on earth that it could be physically done.

Not even in a comic book.

Dad-not-Dad held the big hairy freshly-decapitated head up and took a long cold look at all that was left of my friendly Sasquatch.

"I bet that is a real weight from off of your shoulders," Dad-not-Dad said. "I bet that is a really GREAT cure for a headache."

And then Dad-not-Dad grinned.

It was a terrible joke and a horrifying grin and a part of me was screaming louder than any scream in history had ever been screamed before.

Dad-not-Dad dropped Bigfoot's head in the dirt.

"Sing up the Cave of Tears and put them down in it," Dad-not-Dad broken-glassed in Mannegishi. "I am done with the both of them."

Then he grabbed hold of the pine-needle Warren-cocoon.

"I have got what I came for," Dad-not-Dad said.

And then he walked away dragging the Warren-cocoon behind him in the dirt like some sort of a funky pine-needle and dead leaf security blanket.

"Fine," I said. "Just fine."

Chapter Thirty Two – Singing Up The Cave of Tears

THE MANNEGISHI SANG to the hill that we stood beside.

It wasn't a pretty song.

It sounded a lot like their language but only worse. A whole lot worse. It sounded like a murder of angry crows cursing at broken glass in the middle of a cymbal solo on top of the rustiest tin roof in the universe.

Loud, nasty and cracked in two where the pieces ought to fit.

I could see a raven's head forming in the mountain. I could see the big old black feathered cowl and the big old jowl in the throat and I could see a pair of cold eyes like flat black river stones. At first it looked as if the head was made out of mountain and trees and shadow but then as the Mannegishi continued their long and ugly singing it began to look as if the mountain was made out of raven.

The sunlight streaming down over my shoulder should have felt warm and comforting but I shivered just the same.

The beak of the raven in the mountain opened like a welcoming doorway and I could see a cave hiding inside of the gaping beak.

Several of the Mannegishi escorted Coyote into the cave. Coyote didn't seem to want to fight them. I guess those raven feathers he was chewing on had somehow taken all of the fight out of him – even after he had his mouth stitched shut with a bone needle.

Another couple of Mannegishi carried Bigfoot's head into the cave.

Then they came for me.

"Fine," I said. "Just fine."

Only it wasn't fine.

I felt like I was caught in one of those crazy nasty dreams that you sometimes have. You know that kind of dream where you can't stop yourself from doing something no matter how stupid or bad or dangerous that something really was.

I should have run - but I just walked along, hanging onto one of the Mannegishi's extended hand like I was three years old and hanging onto my Mom's hand while she walked me safely across a busy intersection.

I wondered to myself what was going to happen in the cave.

Was the cave going to chew us up and eat us?

I supposed it might have. The cave kind of looked like a big old wide-open mouth, all hungry and ready chew, and after seeing lake dragons and giant islands and a birch tree Spirit Bear I was just about ready to believe that anything was possible.

I walked inside.

I wondered to myself what the Raven really wanted with Warren's cocoon.

It wasn't like the Warren cocoon was all that pretty to look at.

I supposed he could have used the Warren cocoon as a throw cushion or maybe to stop up a leak in a plaster wall.

I wondered to myself if Old Shuck had got away from the pursuing Mannegishi hunters.

I hoped that he had.

I wondered all of these things while I walked into the Cave of Tears but mostly I just wondered if I was ever going to walk out of this cave alive again.

And then the Mannegishi sang their ugly song one more time and the cave closed its mouth leaving me and a sewed-up

Coyote and Bigfoot's decapitated head huddled alone together in the darkness of the Cave of Tears.

It wasn't exactly a comfortable sort of situation.

I would like to tell you that I was brave and courageous about the whole thing - but a fellow's last words on earth probably ought not to be a lie.

Chapter Thirty Three – This is One Of Those Kinds Of Stories

DID YOU EVER hear a story that you told yourself you would never forget?

Did you ever swear that you were going to remember something only you didn't?

Did you ever set out to commit every single detail of something you had heard into the lockbox of your memory – only to find out that your lockbox had rusted shut a long time ago and you had already lost the key to the lockbox an d besides - your mother had already thrown that lockbox last Saturday in a fit of sudden Spring cleaning.

That was how my whole life suddenly seemed.

Everything that I thought I knew about my Dad had somehow turned into a full-blown lie.

He wasn't a hero.

He hadn't died in Afghanistan.

He didn't even like dogs.

Besides all of that, he had clearly demonstrated a very bad habit of pulling heads off of dropkicked and speared-to-death Sasquatches.

I closed my eyes and did my very best to push past all of the stories that I had told myself about my Dad.

It was hard.

It was a little like fighting fog.

I had been telling myself those stories for so many years they were all I really had to believe in, but maybe they were nothing more than lies I had been telling myself.

What did I really remember about my Dad?

Not that much, come to think of it.

Dad was always somewhere else.

I looked down at that Bigfoot head that was still lying in the dirt beside me just exactly where Dad's pet Mannegishi had dragged and dropped it.

I was chained to the side of the cage that Coyote was locked inside. I don't really know where the Mannegishi had found a cage like that out here in the wilderness. Maybe they had made it out of magic. Maybe they had found it in a jailhouse yard sale.

I don't know.

I tried not to stare at Bigfoot's head.

The flies were buzzing around that rotting head-meat like they were telling themselves long bedtime stories about fat and grease and garbage and decaying Sasquatch heads.

I'm not saying that it was pretty.

The daylight slipped away like sand running out of a broken hourglass. Darkness tucked in over the land and I closed my eyes and thought about sleep.

"No," a voice said. "Don't look away."

It was Warren's voice.

"Don't you EVER dare look away again," Warren's voice said. "You keep your eyes wide open and you will live to tell."

I looked down in the direction that the voice was coming from.

I knew what I was going to see before I even saw it.

It was Bigfoot who was talking but it was my Stepdad Warren's voice that was coming from out of Bigfoot's talking mouth. Worse yet, I could see Warren's beady little eyes staring out from Bigfoot's big shaggy eyeholes.

"Whatever happens," Bigfoot/Warren went on. "Don't you ever dare to look away again, not even for a minute. Remember, life is like a movie with no reruns ever. You don't want to blink. You don't want to miss a single shining moment of it."

"I'm not blinking," I said sincerely. "My eyes are stuck wide open."

It was fear that was keeping my eyes open – but I guess that was good enough for Bigfoot/Warren.

"Good," Bigfoot/Warren said. "Keep them that way."

"So are you really actually dead?" I asked. "That would definitely be an important thing for me to know in this particular situation."

"Well that's a whole other story," Bigfoot/Warren replied. "But I think that by now you really ought to know that stories never die so long as people remember to tell them."

"That's still not an answer," I said.

"You're looking at me," Bigfoot/Warren said. "And I am talking to you. Is there really anything else that you need to know?"

I blinked my eyes.

I guess I shouldn't have blinked because all of a sudden I was just looking at a dead severed Sasquatch head.

I guess I shouldn't have blinked.

"Is there anything else you need to know?" a voice from behind me asked.

I looked around, startled.

It was Coyote who was talking to me.

"What happened to that thread that was sticking your mouth together?" I asked. "And what about those raven feathers that were keeping you all cheerful and dumb?"

"Those raven feathers weren't really keeping me cheerful and dumb on account of they were nothing more than a couple of crow feathers I grabbed out of a passing murder of crows," Coyote explained. "Besides that, you ought to have figured out by now that I am dumb by nature and I absolutely HATE cheerful with a passion."

"Well what about the thread Dad sewed your mouth up shut with?" I asked.

"I tricked him," Coyote said.

"How did you trick him?"

Coyote grinned.

He had two pieces of rope in his hands that he tied together in a knot and then pulled them apart as if the knot had never been tied.

"It's all in how you hold your mouth," Coyote said. "Any magician will tell you that."

Which didn't tell me much at all – and truthfully I could not remember the last time a magician had talked to me - but I guess magicians weren't talkative by nature, especially when it came to revealing their best tricks.

"So what do we do now?" I asked. "Bigfoot is dead and The Prophet is dead and Old Shuck has run off and we're on our own – and no offence but I really don't think that you are good for much of anything at all right now."

"No offence taken," Coyote replied. "I know my own limitations."

"You still haven't answered my question," I pointed out. "What do we do now?"

"How about a story?" Coyote asked. "It is always a good time for that sort of thing."

A story?

Was he trying to kid me?

That freaking did it.

"We're in the middle of a mess like this and you want to stop everything and tell me a story?" I said. "You've got to be ten kinds of ten-kind- stupid to think that I am in any sort of a mood for listening to another boring dumb old story."

"Well, the truth is I'm kind of telling stories so I really wasn't planning on telling you one. What I was figuring was how about if you tell me one?" Coyote asked. "Would you be in the mood for that?"

Wait a minute.

He wanted ME to tell HIM a story?

"What sort of a story would I be able to tell?" I asked him. "All I know is school and video games and maybe a movie or two. I could tell you about the Terminator – the dude comes back to the past from the future to fight a cyborg and save the world until the next sequel? That's a pretty good one, I guess."

Coyote smiled.

"Well, that wasn't that bad of a story for a first attempt – but how about you try telling me a Bigfoot story?" Coyote asked. "Why don't you try telling me about the way that you first met Bigfoot?"

"Why?" I asked. "You were there in the first place."

"Sure," Coyote said. "But I was pretty busy falling off of that magic cloud and sky-diving down onto a rampaging Spirit Bear in a show of manly courage and fortitude to take much note of what you and Bigfoot were actually up to."

I didn't really remember that much courage and fortitude but I didn't have the heart to tell Coyote's story any differently than he had told it to me in the first place.

"Yeah," I said. "But you were there!"

"Is your mouth stuck on repeat?" Coyote asked. "Telling stories is a way to help remember how you got there in the first place. If you tell it right it might even give us some sort of a clue as to how we can get out of this mess."

That didn't make much sense to me at all but nothing had made much sense since that Spirit Bear first climbed out of the birch tree he was hiding inside of.

"All right," I said. "But you had better not interrupt me."

So I started telling my story.

"The first time I saw the Cape Breton Bigfoot he was running straight down the side of a mountain coming right straight at me – and then he spread his arms wide and then he flew - or at least that's what it looked like to me."

I closed my eyes.

It was a little like quiet magic.

All of a sudden I could see the whole story playing out like a movie in the back of my brain , just like it was happening all over again.

So I started to smile, just a little.

"Halfway through mid-charge the Cape Breton Bigfoot tripped his big left foot right over a teetered-up rock," I went on. "Then he flipped over and stuck that same big left foot up into the air behind himself in the wrong direction and pointed his nose straight down towards the dirt and sort of cart wheeled face-first straight down the side of the mountain."

And then I full-out grinned – and for just a half of a half of half of second I felt happy as if all the bad stuff that had been going on was nothing more than a dream in a country that I had never ever been to.

"I'm not saying that it was pretty,"

"Tell it faster," a voice interrupted from somewhere down at my feet. "It's starting to grow on me."

I looked down at where the voice had come from and my jaw dropped two or three times before rolling into the corner of the cave.

I'm STILL not saying that it was pretty.

Chapter Thirty Four – Stories Never Truly Die

"**WHAT ARE YOU** waiting for," the voice at my feet asked. "Don't tell me that you have already forgotten how to tell my story?"

It was Bigfoot that was talking to me.

Now if this was some kind of a horror zombie monster movie it probably wouldn't have bothered me one little bit but there is something more than just a little bit disturbing about having a Sasquatch's decapitated head talking at you like you ought to know better.

I stammered a little.

I'm not sure I made any kind of sense.

"What the, holy, oh my, what the, golly," was about how it came out along with a half-a-dozen startled grunts and at least one dry spit take.

"I keep telling you things and you just don't listen," one-ninth-of-a-Bigfoot said to me. "I get the feeling that you are either totally stupid, half-deaf or maybe you just don't quite understand the workings of the Queen's own English."

"But you're dead," I finally spat out. "I saw you die."

"I'm not dead," one-ninth-of-a-Bigfoot said. "I'm a story. Stories don't really die – not the way that people die – not so long as other people remember to tell them out loud."

"But he pulled your head off," I said. "I saw it happen."

"Sure he pulled my head off," one-ninth-or-maybe-even-one-tenth-(because-math-was-never-my-strong-point)-of-a-Bigfoot said. "But that isn't really all there is to me. All that my head and body are is nothing more than a wrapping for the whole entire story of me. My memories and my legends and the things that I have done and the things that people THINK I've done – that's the real meat of me. That's where I live and breathe. Decapitation doesn't do a thing to somebody built like I am."

I chewed on that concept for just a little bit.

As theories go it was pretty hard to swallow.

"So if I tell your story out loud you are going to grow back?" I asked. "Belly, arms, legs, feet and all?"

"If you tell it well enough," one-ninth-or-tenth-or-maybe-even-one-sixteenth-of-a-Bigfoot replied. "You were starting well enough at the beginning. I could feel the spark burning behind your words but then you got all bogged down in disbelief and wonder and worrying about a simple little thing like a Sasquatch head re-growing itself and you went and forgot just which way were going."

I chewed on that notion as well, slowly thinking his words over.

"I think I got it," I said, not really sure but figuring that if I said I got it often enough then maybe I could full myself into figuring out just what he was talking about.

And then – because I couldn't figure out what else I ought to do - I just started back into telling that first story and I told just as strong and as true as I could manage to. I told it straight out and I added a little bit along the way. In my story Coyote didn't just fall off of a cloud. In my story he came para-gliding on a great red and orange and sunrise colored para-glider with bells and whistles and big red fire horns and a couple of shotgun laser gun turrets mounted on each of the para-glider wings.

I took a glance at Coyote but he didn't seem to be listening at all. He was just staring vaguely into space, like he was dreaming.

I tell you, he was missing himself one heck of a story.

Hey – you go ahead and try sitting in a dark raven cave in Labrador with nothing but a severed Sasquatch head and a stitched-up-lip Coyote to keep you company and see if YOUR imagination doesn't run a little wild on you.

The funny thing was, as I continued to tell my story I could see that Bigfoot was slowly beginning to grow. First I could see his neck growing out of his severed head like the root of a big fat old dandelion.

"That's the thing about telling stories," Bigfoot said.

I could see his great big yellow funky-smelling Sasquatch teeth grinning up at me about as bright as a full-sized set of freshly-Colgated light bulbs.

"After a while," Coyote said. "They begin to grow on you."

"A little like mildew," Bigfoot said. "Or maybe even like creeping mold."

"Or a bad case of the measles," Coyote added.

And son of a gun, after a while, those stories did just that.

They grew and they grew.

And so did Bigfoot.

Chapter Thirty Five – Out of the Cave and into the Light

BY THE TIME I had finished telling the story of how I had first met Bigfoot and Coyote, Bigfoot had grown himself a brand new body and the stumps of his legs and arms.

Now mind you they did not exactly LOOK like legs and arms. They looked more like those stubby little eyes that grow on a potato if you leave it for too long in the cupboard, until it begins to sprout.

"Just keep on talking," Bigfoot encouraged. "Keep on telling."

I kept thinking about all of those stories that my stepdad Warren had tried to tell me and I kept wishing that I had actually listened to a few of them – but I kept on telling my stories just as hard as I could manage to.

I told about how Bigfoot had managed to single-handedly capture and granny knot the mighty Great Lake Dragons. I told how he had subdued Nanna Bijou and had compelled him to tell Bigfoot just exactly how we could track down Raven. I told how Bigfoot had managed to take Old Shuck down in two out of three falls without a bit of help from either myself, The Prophet, or Coyote.

Oh sure, I was exaggerating in places and I was outright lying in other places but none of the lying and exaggerating really mattered at all - because when it came right down to it I was doing just exactly what every storyteller in the world has ever done before me.

I was stretching the truth and making it shine just a little bit brighter.

Embellishing, some folks would call it.

Others might say I was falsifying data.

Some might even call it lying.

Why not?

Stephen King gets paid ALL kinds of money to make stuff up like this.

So do some politicians that I have heard some grown-ups I know talking about.

I had always hated English class – ESPECIALLY The creative writing part of it. Back then I had always thought that writing and telling stories was stupid and dumb and boring – but now I could see there was a real point behind it and not only that – but it was really kind of fun.

Why shouldn't I try and make use of my flexible rubber imagination and my ability to make things up to help myself and to help my friends and to help me get the heck out of this funky old raven cave?

So I kept on telling my homemade Bigfoot story right on up to this point that you are hearing right now – and then, when I had run out of road to run on I started to make stories up. I told Bigfoot a story of how he had beaten King Kong himself in an arm wrestling match, thanks to a little trick that Coyote had pulled off involving a feather duster, some sneezing powder, a banana and a rubber chicken.

Then I told how Bigfoot had created the Northern Lights using nothing but a slide projector, some colored cellophane and a half a dozen tins of paint that he had peeled from off of an abandoned church in the wrong end of a British Columbia ghost town directly after he had finished beating up all of the ghost town's ghosts.

I was halfway through a story involving Bigfoot, Ogopogo, Superman and Hulk Hogan – and I really wasn't sure just where I was going to go with a cast as varied as that one – when

Bigfoot stood back on up. He looked a little wobbly and some parts of his arms and legs still seemed to be growing and I wasn't really certain if I had got the color right in his fur – but he stood up just the same.

"It's really good to see you," I said. "I was afraid that you were going to quit while you were a head."

"It's good to see you," Bigfoot replied. "But I knew that you would come through for me in a pinch."

"You never doubted did you?" I said. "After all, I am a storyteller."

I was thinking of Warren when I said that.

I was thinking about all of the stories that he had told me in the few years that I had known him. I was thinking about how much of himself he put into those stories and how much of those stories he had kept trying to put into my thinking.

And all I could do for him was to turn away and make fun of him and do my very best not to listen.

How stupid could I have ever been?

I made a promise to myself – there in the heart of the Labrador Cave of Tears – that I was going to get that Warren cocoon back from Raven and I was going to sit down and tell Warren's stories back to him to show him that I had been listening all along. I was going to tell stories to that Warren cocoon until the cows came home and gave milk and then jumped into a meat grinder and made hamburgers out of themselves.

It was a promise.

It was a promise that I swore that I was going to keep.

"So how do we get out of here?" I asked Bigfoot. "I've got some deep meaningful Raven payback to grab hold of."

"You're starting to really dislike that bird fellow, aren't you?" Coyote asked me.

"Dislike is a kind of a strong word to use," I said. "Let's just say that I intend to pluck him and put him into a pot full of noodles and then I will sing Hank Snow songs to him while he boils himself down into a bowl full of raven noodle soup."

I had to grin at that.

As death threats go, it was pretty awesomely colorful.

"You tell a lot of good stories, kid," Bigfoot said. "Now let me tell you how I am going to escape out of this cave."

"I hope it isn't going to be a long story," I said. "Because I am feeling just a little bit impatient right about now."

"It will be a real short story," Bigfoot said, drawing his big right fist about six inches behind his big hairy right ear.

"It will start about here," Bigfoot said. "About seven inches behind my right ear."

"I could have sworn it was six inches," I said.

"Don't bother me with details or mathematics," Bigfoot corrected. "My story starts here and it ends right about HERE!"

He leaned forward into a beautiful right cross that hit the closed-up mouth of the Raven's Cave of Tears like a half a dozen nuclear missiles rolled into one.

"POW!!!" Bigfoot, Coyote and me shouted in unison – and there were not enough exclamation marks in the entire universe to punctuationally demonstrate the power and the impact of Bigfoot's big right hand.

The mouth of the Raven's Cave of Tears opened up and barfed out boulders and stones and pebbles and bat poop and cave beetles and them funky little lizards that sometimes crawl on the walls of a cave.

We stepped out into the daylight, blinking and squinting from the glare of the sudden sunshine and the dust that Bigfoot's thunderous thump had stirred up.

He put his big hand against my chest.

"Hold on a minute," Bigfoot said. "I need to make me a long-distance call."

Then Bigfoot took three slow deliberate steps forward.

I watched as his eyes glazed over as if he was trying to squint hard into some sort of middle-distance sandstorm , trying hard to focus on something that wasn't really there.

Then Bigfoot leaned back and he opened his mouth wide enough to swallow a medium sized steam roller. Then he took a great big deep breath and then he yelled about as loud of a yell as was humanly possible for a nine foot tall Sasquatch.

"RAVEN!!!"

The earth shook a little.

And then Bigfoot shouted again.

"COME HERE!!!!"

I saw a few trees lean just a tiny bit away from the shout.

And then he shouted a third time.

"I WANT YOU, NOW!!!!!"

The clouds shook a little in the sky.

I am pretty sure I actually might have heard a dozen or so black bears faint just a little, somewhere about three miles west of the Quebec/Ontario border line.

The sky clouded over.

It was almost as if I had blinked and while I was in mid-blink and wondering somebody had stolen that bright blue Labrador sky and then had replaced it with the promise of a thunderstorm, it had happened that fast.

I felt a slow chill creep down my backbone, winding up about halfway down my left little toe.

I blinked for real.

Somewhere in the middle of my mid-blink my Dad appeared.

Dad-not-Dad.

Chapter Thirty Six – Triple Somersaults All Over The Place

IT WAS LIKE something out of one of those old John Wayne movies.

Dad-not-Dad stood at one side of the clearing and Bigfoot stood at the other.

"I thought that I had seen the last of you," Dad-not-Dad said to Bigfoot. "Aren't you supposed to be dead by now?"

"Not hardly," Bigfoot said.

Dad-not-Dad shook his head.

"That's the problem with things nowadays," Dad-not-Dad said. "Time was, you'd decapitate a fellow and he would have the common decency to STAY decapitated."

"That's your story," Bigfoot said. "That's not my story."

Dad-not-Dad turned his head and let his gaze fall on me.

I felt a chill run through me like I had gargled ice cold glacier water in the middle of a March blizzard.

"I am thinking that you probably had some help," Dad-not-Dad said. "I am thinking that boy might have been telling stories on you."

His eyes hardened just a little.

"That's the Teller in you, coming out," Dad-not-Dad said, looking down at the Warren-cocoon lying there in the dirt beside him.

"We're not related," I said. "Warren's just my stepdad. Let him go. He isn't anything to you."

Dad-not-Dad laughed at that.

"You've been listening to the wrong kind of stories," Dad-not-Dad said. "The fact is that fellow in that holding-cocoon has done his very best to take care of you."

He had?

"You knew the true story all along," Dad-not-Dad said. "You were just too busy talking to stop and listen to what your ears were trying to tell you."

I was?

He wasn't carrying a gun – but I still couldn't escape the feeling that he was just about to pull one from out of his sleeve and shoot me dead, maybe three or four times fast.

"Do you know what I like to do to boys who tell too many stories?" Dad-not-Dad asked.

Bigfoot took a slow shaky step forward.

"Over my dead body," Bigfoot said.

Out of all the phrases in the dictionary WHY did he have to pick that one?

Dad-not-Dad turned his gaze back onto Bigfoot.

"Oh I can arrange that particular development easily enough," Dad-not-Dad said. "And this time I guarantee it'll stay stuck."

"What about me?" Coyote asked, stepping out of the shadows of the cave. "It seems to me that you and I have some business to discuss."

Dad-not-Dad just grinned.

"You don't really think that I am actually worried about what you might do or not do, little brother?" Dad-not-Dad said to Coyote.

"You ought to be worried," Coyote replied. "I might have learned a trick or two since we last spoke."

Dad-not-Dad smiled sadly.

"Funny," he said. "I don't think I ever remember speaking to you. In fact, if I had to sum your entire life story in one single word I would have to go with unmemorable."

Coyote just growled.

"And as for you," Dad-not-Dad went on, shifting his gaze back to Bigfoot. "Back from the dead or not, you just don't look all that ready to be talking about teaching me any sort of a lesson."

He had a point.

Bigfoot did NOT look half as tough as he did when I first met him. I guess being decapitated and speared to death will do that to a fellow – no matter how strong and hairy he starts out as.

"Enough talk," Bigfoot growled.

He ran straight at Dad-not-Dad who just stood there waiting calmly as several hundred pounds of enraged Sasquatch charged in his general direction.

Bigfoot built up speed.

Dad-not-Dad still did not move.

And then at the very last moment before impact Dad-not-Dad stepped to one side, leaving his foot leaned out. It was the oldest schoolyard trick in the book and it worked perfectly. Bigfoot hit Dad-not-Dad's stuck-out foot with his own snowshoe-sized monstrosity and performed a wondrous triple somersault in mid-air before crashing to the dirt.

Dad-not-Dad looked down at his fallen opponent and shook his head sadly.

"You really aren't up to this sort of thing, are you?" Dad-not-Dad said. "Maybe you should have brought along some help with you?"

It wasn't Bigfoot's fault. He was still recovering from being decapitated and poked with spears about a hundred times or so. Still, I blamed myself for his weakness. I should have told his stories longer and stronger.

I should have done better than I had.

"He doesn't need any help," Coyote howled. "He's got me!"

I had almost forgotten that Coyote was still standing beside me – only he wasn't standing anymore. He took off running, straight at Dad-not-Dad, and for just a half of a half moment I thought that I was about to see a repeat performance of Bigfoot's wondrous triple somersault of death.

Dad-not-Dad just stood there waiting.

I guess he was figuring the same thing as I was.

Only Coyote wasn't interested in attempting Bigfoot's triple somersault of death.

About halfway to touchdown Coyote spread his arms wide like a big funny-smelling shaggy eagle.

And then he flew.

Chapter Thirty Seven – A Major League World Class Grade A Butt-Kicking

I know.

I know.

Way back when I first started telling you this story I already TOLD you how it looked as if Bigfoot flew – way back when he was running down the Cape Breton mountainside, pointed directly at that Spirit Bear.

Only Coyote didn't just LOOK like he was flying.

Coyote spread his arms wide and all at once a wonderful red and orange and sunrise colored para-glider wings – complete with bells and whistles and big red fire horns and a couple of shotgun laser gun turrets mounted on each of the para-glider wings – spread out from beneath his arms.

I recognized those wings.

Those were the very same pair of imaginary para-glider wings that I had given Coyote in my Bigfoot story, way back in the Cave of Tears.

I guess Coyote had been listening to my story all along, back in that cave.

I made a mental note to apologize to him – assuming we lived through this long enough to tell about it.

"I told you that I had learned a trick or two," Coyote howled.

He soared upwards into the Labrador sky, banking a little to the left and then pointing his nose upwards before climbing skyward.

I guess that I had told my story well enough for him to evolve his own personal mythology out of my imagination.

You learn something new every day, I guess.

Who would have thought that there would have been so much power hidden in one seventeen year old imagination?

Coyote continued upwards.

He clearly was enjoying his brand new wings.

I was awfully glad to see that he did – especially since I had gone and invented them like I did – but I still would have rather seen him use those brand new wings and those laser gun turrets on Dad-not-Dad.

It turned out my wish was not long in coming true.

I watched closely as Coyote climbed up past the few curious seagulls who were drifting by. He climbed so high that I had to squint to see him.

For a moment I was worried that he was just going to fly away and leave me standing here, looking stupid.

Then Coyote sort of yawed himself around, turning and flattening out and sort of hanging a long slow somersault of a turn in mid-air and then roaring down directly towards my Dad-not-Dad – those laser gun turrets blasting in a full-out strafing run.

"Do it," I said. "Blast him to pieces."

By now I guess that you can see that I had come to think of that Dad-not-Dad as something or someone that was definitely bad news.

He wasn't going to look after me.

He wasn't going to talk to me like my real Dad should have talked to me.

I had decided that whatever else happened it would be a really good thing if someone – either Coyote or Bigfoot or even Old

Shuck, if he ever came back – laid a major league world class serious grade A butt-kicking on Mister Dad-not-Dad.

I grinned, figuring that I was just about to see that very thing.

It turned out I was right.

Coyote bore down on Dad-not-Dad, those roaring lasers making an absolutely horrifying mess of Labrador. It turned out that Coyote could not aim any better than all of those thousands of Star Wars Imperial Stormtroopers who had never managed to hit Luke Skywalker in three straight movies.

Coyote blasted trees and tore up the grass and incinerated a half an acre of blueberry bushes and flambéed an innocently bystanding inukshuk – but as near as I could tell he hadn't laid so much as a single scorch-mark on Dad-not-Dad.

And then – before Coyote could work on improving his aim - Dad-not-Dad swung his right arm out in mid-air like he was trying to karate chop a mosquito. A huge solid-looking black feather shot out like some crazy bird's idea of a ninja throwing star shot out from out of Dad-not-Dad's extended hand and flew like a jet-propelled arrow aimed directly at Coyote.

"Ha!" Coyote barked, as he easily banked out of the flying feather's path. "Is that the best that you can do?"

Coyote grinned about as hard as a story could ever grin, but I wasn't all that certain that Coyote was about to deeply regret what he had just said.

Dad-not-Dad swung his left arm out in a similar mid-air karate chop and about twenty black feathers shot out from his fingertips – catching Coyote in mid-bank, still grinning.

I watched in horror as about eight of those feathers tore into Coyote's hide.

I guess Dad-not-Dad aimed a whole better than a stormtrooper ever did.

"I know a few tricks, too," Dad-not-Dad said – with a really mean sort of a grin.

Coyote crashed to the ground.

Bigfoot was down.

Coyote was down.

Old Shuck was nowhere in sight.

I was left all alone.

"No what am I going to do with you, boy?" Dad-not-Dad asked.

I expected that he would think of something soon enough.

Only I did not give him the chance.

"How about if I tell YOU a story?" I asked.

Then I took my first step and began to walk towards Dad-not-Dad.

Chapter Thirty Eight – One Last Dad Story

Okay – so you have got to stop for just a moment and try to comprehend just how unbelievably stupid my next move appeared – even to me.

Here I was – a seventeen year old kid armed with nothing more than a somewhat questionable attitude and a real sense of somebody-has-got-to-do-something-about-this and here I was – getting set to play flinch-chicken with a living breathing legend.

Now when I say "legend" I am not just talking about the fact that Dad-not-Dad was most likely the Raven himself, in disguise.

I am sorry. Did I just spoil that for you? I was pretty certain that you had already figured things out about six or seven chapters back – but if I did spoil it just promise me that you will do your best to squint over my mistakes and forgive me for blurting out.

You see, it didn't really impress me all that much – the thought that I was attempting to face down the Raven.

I'm seventeen, remember?

To me, a raven is nothing more than a bird.

But this Raven looked just like my real Dad.

Talk about your living legends.

Worse yet, I wasn't even sure if he hadn't been my real Dad all along.

I mean just think about it.

How could I know for certain that my real Dad hadn't been Raven in disguise all along? I mean, my Mom probably wouldn't have known. That sort of thing happens all of the time. Just think back to all of the times that you heard somebody on television who has just found out that his next door neighbor was actually a chainsaw massacring serial killer say something along the lines of "Well, I guess I never knew that person as well as I thought I did."

Just try and think about all of the times that YOU said that very same thing – even if you did not say it out loud to anyone but just to yourself.

People are puzzles that way.

We are complicated mechanisms.

Just when you think that you have got a certain person all figured out they go and they change on you and you have to go and start that whole figuring-out process all over again from the beginning.

I kept walking towards Dad-not-Dad.

I tried my hardest to remember some of the music from all of those John Wayne gunfighter movies that Warren had made me watch – but all I could think of was the theme music from Sponge Bob Square Pants – and you just can't look all that tough humming to yourself.

So instead I did the very next best thing.

I opened up my mouth and said something.

"I've got a story to tell you," I said to Dad-not-Dad.

"Ha!" Dad-not-Dad laughed out loud. "You came all this way out here just to tell me a story? That's got to be one of the saddest things I have ever heard."

"Are you done?" I asked. "Or are you just afraid to hear me tell my story?"

The way I figured things, it never hurts to throw a little double-dare into any argument that you are trying hard to win.

"I am not afraid of anything you can dish out," Dad-not-Dad said. "But if I even think that you are going to start telling a

Bigfoot story or a Coyote story or even a story about a big footed coyote then I am going to pull your tongue out and feed it to the rats."

Truthfully, I had thought for about a half of a half of a half minute about doing just that – but the way I saw it Dad-not-Dad had already proven that he could lay a beat-down on both Coyote and Bigfoot without even breaking a sweat.

So I had to find another plan.

"Go ahead and tell your story if you feel you have to," Dad-not-Dad said. "I'll most likely pull your tongue out anyway, directly after you are done."

It is awfully hard to tell a story when you are trying your hardest to keep your mouth closed and your tongue safely in your mouth – but I managed it, just the same.

"Have you ever heard the story about The Invisible Man?" I asked.

Dad-not-Dad snorted in derision.

"I not only heard the story," Dad-not-Dad said. "But I saw the movie and read the book and you had better start telling me something new because my patience has about the limitations of a melting bowl of ice cream on a hot summer day."

"This isn't any story that you heard," I told him. "This is the story of the Invisible Dad."

And then I started telling.

"Once upon a time," I said. "There was a woman and she married a man who told her that he was a hero but he wasn't. He lied to that woman. Every time that she started counting on him to be somewhere where she needed him to be he was somewhere else. After a while she began to think of him as being her invisible husband."

Dad-not-Dad was still listening but he did not look as if he was really enjoying what he was hearing – namely, the truth.

"So then one day a son was born and that invisible husband grew about fifty more shades of indistinct. Now every time that son went looking for his father that dad was always somewhere else. After a time that son began to think about his father as being something more along the lines of the Invisible Dad."

Now Dad-not-Dad was doing his best to look in another direction.

"He was a little like some kind of a parental vampire," I went on. "Every time that the sun came out and the boy looked around that Invisible Dad was nowhere to be seen. Now that bothered the boy's mother because she sort of grew the feeling that it was somehow all her fault that the Dad did not want to be anywhere close to his family."

I got a little choked up while I was telling this story but I told myself that it was a little like a spoon full of bitter cough syrup. I just had to open up and get it over with.

"So she began to tell her son stories about her Invisible Dad," I went on. "She told how the son that his Dad was really a hero and that he HAD to be away and that he would have loved to have been able to hang around with his son but he had way too many duties that he simply had to take care of."

I swallowed a lump that was growing inside of my throat.

I badly wanted to spit but I was worried that Dad-not-Dad might take that as an excuse to rip out my tongue like he had already threatened to.

"After a while," I continued to tell. "That boy began to believe in all of those stories that his Mom kept on telling him about his Invisible Dad. Worse yet, the boy began telling brand new stories that he made up himself and after a while of telling himself these brand new Invisible Dad stories the very worst thing in the world happened."

I looked up and stared directly into Dad-not-Dad's eyes.

They were grey.

I'm not talking color, you understand. I am talking texture. Dad-not-Dad's eyes had somehow taken on the character of smoky grey, like the lonely grey smoke that winds its way up from out of the ashes of a forgotten campfire.

"The boy began to believe in his Invisible Dad," I went on. "Which was the worst thing that he could ever think of doing."

I was telling that story to myself as much as anyone and a part of me wanted to laugh.

Another part of me wanted to cry.

The biggest part of me just did not care any longer.

"Then one day somebody else came into that boy's mother's life. It was another man and he met her when she needed help and he was kind enough to try to help and he wasn't afraid one little bit of accidentally looking stupid," I went on. "As crazy and as stupid as it sounded that other guy that had come into Mom's life had just wanted to help."

It almost looked to me as if Dad-not-Dad was beginning to entirely turn into that very same campfire smoke. I could see him wavering just a little and it almost looked to me as if I could see through some of the places where I shouldn't have been able to see.

"He tried to fix her tire while she called for AAA," I said. "He tried to dance with her and he stepped on her foot and fractured it and he sat by her bed for six straight weeks, nursing her with grilled cheese sandwiches and tomato soup. He always remembered to put that dab of butter into the middle of the bowl of tomato soup, just the way that she liked it."

Dad-not-Dad opened his mouth.

Then he closed it again.

As far as I could tell no words had fallen out in between.

"Something else I remember," I went on. "Was the way that other guy was always there for Mom. The way he smiled at her when he said "good morning" like seeing her there to smile at was the single biggest most important part of making that morning a good morning. I remember him always standing up from his chair at the dinner table for Mom – even when she was just bringing the potatoes – like she was some kind of royalty."

Dad-not-Dad was rumbling to himself now, like he was gargling boulders in the back of his throat.

"That other guy's name was Warren," I said. "And he was good to me too – even though I was a bit of a jerk to him."

"I'll be sure to look him up the next time I'm on Facebook," Dad-not-Dad said.

He was trying to make a comeback – trying to tell a joke and maybe get back to telling his own story and getting back up on top of this situation but I wasn't going to give him the chance.

I kept telling my story like it was the very last story that I would tell on this good earth.

"He was good to me, too," I repeated. "He taught me how to throw a football and how to do mathematics and how to run like the wind."

I could see Warren now, standing there in thin mid-air, hovering behind Dad-not-Dad. I don't know if he was some sort of a spirit come back or if he was just becoming a story himself or if I was just imagining the whole situation – but I did not let that keep me from keeping on telling.

"You keep on telling that story if you want to," Dad-not-Dad said. "But the truth is you have been living with the *Se'skwetew* for too long now. This Warren-thing means nothing and you ought to know that. You are better off living with the memory of me."

"Your memory is important to me, Dad," I said. "But that doesn't mean I can't have more than one memory and more than one story. My memory of my Dad as being my hero hasn't changed and the fact that he really was nothing more than a fellow who couldn't figure out how to stick around long enough to actually get to his son hasn't changed and the fact that Warren is trying his very best to be there for me and my Mom doesn't change either."

"So what has changed?" Dad-not-Dad asked.

"What has changed," I said. "is the fact that I have finally figured out just WHO you really are."

"Who?" Dad-not-Dad asked.

"No," I said. "You are not an owl. That is not the kind of bird that you are at all, is it? And you sure as shooting aren't my Dad."

"Then who am I?" Not-Dad asked the space about two or three inches above my hairline on account of he suddenly could not look me in the eye.

Now, it was my turn to smile.

"Come on out," I said. "You are not fooling anyone anymore."

My smile widened into a big old grin.

"Come on out, Raven," I said.

Chapter Thirty Nine – A Long Midnight Feather Duster

The smile was the very first thing that slid off of Not-Dad's face.

Actually the smile kind of peeled off just a little bit at a time, like a Band-Aid that had been stuck onto somebody's too-wet skin. The smile slid down Not-Dad's chin and then it slid off into mid-air and then hung there about halfway to the ground and then I realized that that smile was nothing more than the scrap of a dried-up willow leaf and then it drifted down to the dirt.

The next thing that fell off was Not-Dad's eyes, sliding down his smoky grey cheekbone like a pair of see-through snails. They blinked at me in mid-air and then fell to the dirt like a pair of insincere tear drops. I almost chuckled when I realized that the jet black pupils of his eyes had been nothing more than a couple of sun-dried blackberries.

I watched as that great orange beak slowly pushed out from the plane of his face and his lips peeled back from that beak like a pair of freshly-skinned river eels. I watched as dirty black feathers poked out from his skin and I could smell something that reeked a little like old cheese and sour milk. I saw his arms spread back like they were being pulled by a hidden master puppeteer and a pair of shiny long black wings grew out from his shoulders and his elbows and his fingertips like he was wearing a long feathery midnight shadow.

Then his shoes melted away and the blue of his faded denim jeans washed out into pale winter sky tones before fading into nothing as a pair of mean and angry raven legs and talons pushed out from his hipbones to take their place.

"You have got a pair of good eyes," Raven said to me. "I wonder if I ought to beak them out of your head and see just what they really would taste like."

Now I had faced way too many bullies in my life to let a big old overgrown mynah bird put the scare into me – even if he was actually scaring me half to death.

I wasn't going to let him know.

"I would not recommend that," I said. "You would probably choke on them. I have got a pretty hard old stare and it gets worse when I am looking at crows."

"I am a Raven," Dad-not-Dad said.

"I know who you are," I said. "I made you up out of wishful thinking and now I am no longer afraid of you and I am no longer afraid to stand here on my own two feet and I reckon that you might as well just blow away like the smoke from a birthday candle. I have outgrown you and I no longer have any kind use for the story you keep trying to tell me."

"That's all that you have left," Raven said. "Is nothing but old boring stories."

"That's fine by me," I said. "I'll stick with my stories."

"The truth is better than that," Raven said. "only I can tell you the truth."

I thought about that.

There was an awful lot about this whole situation that I did not understand.

I knew that Dad had been real and I knew that he had married Mom and I knew that he and Mom had done whatever parents do to make children and they had made me. But then I knew that Dad had spent every minute after that trying to stay away from me and my Mom.

I don't know if he was the Raven or if the Raven was just trying to pretend that I was the son of a Raven.

I don't really if I ever know.

I just know that being with Mom makes me happy and Warren makes Mom happy which makes me even happier and three kinds of happy adds up to an awful lot of goodness and if I live to be a hundred and three it won't really matter if I ever find out the truth of what the Raven really was trying to tell me.

"The truth is cold," I told him. "I'll stick with my stories every time. A good story is like a good campfire. It keeps you warm at night and it teaches you how to dream and there are way too many facts in this world already. I'd rather dream awhile and let the facts take care of themselves."

"You don't know the truth of it," Raven said.

"I know most of it," I said. "And what I don't know I can always guess at and if my guessing is wrong – well, I can live with that too. A fellow doesn't need to know everything there is to know. Mostly all that is worth believing in are the things that are mostly unbelievable."

"What kind things are those?" Raven asked.

"Things like love and peace and happiness and the way that happy endings seem to happen when you most figure that they won't," I said. "All of those rules that people tell us – well those aren't anything more than stories and stories are sometimes the most important truth of all."

Raven just sneered at me.

"Suit your own self," Raven said.

Then he spread his wings wide open – so wide that if the sun hadn't been going like it was I was pretty certain that he could have blocked out the sun with one single shrug - and then, just as he was about to take wing the Ghost of Sam Steele reached out from the shadows of the Labrador wilderness and caught that Raven by the scruff of its black feathered neck.

"You have the right to remain silent," the Ghost of Sam Steele said. "In fact I would most sincerely prefer it if you would stay that way."

Raven cracked his wings backwards, throwing the Ghost of Sam Steele down into the dirt. Then he kicked some of that dirt into Sam Steele's eyes and then he laughed a mean little laugh and spread his wings again and was just taking flight when Nanna Bijou – the Sleeping Giant of Thunder Bay – now wide awake and bigger than ten mountains all rolled into one – swatted Raven like a Labrador black fly, flattening that Trickster God down into something that looked a steamrollered pancake shadow.

"Anything you say or do can and will be held against you," the Ghost of Sam Steele went on. "Assuming you actually live to survive your apprehension."

A bird flew overhead and dropped something sticky and white upon Raven's forehead, just to add insult to injury.

I could hear the thin crackling sounds of raw electric guitars, jackhammers, bagpipes and three guys yelling MISUNDERSTOOD-NUMBER-TWENTY-THREE, MISUNDERSTOOD-NUMBER-TWENTY-THREE, MISUNDERSTOOD-NUMBER-TWENTY-THREE bleeding out from the poorly fitted headphones that I had given Nanna Bijou.

He was still wearing them, playing them as loudly as he could, and grinning so hard I swear he might have inadvertently broken a couple of his own teeth.

Raven looked up at that big old Mountain God and he rolled his eyes so loudly I swore that I could hear them rattling like a cup full of dice.

And then all of a sudden Old Shuck was standing on top of Raven – with all of his great purple Death Dog weight pressed upon Raven's shoulder bones with all of Old Shuck's great purple Death Dog weight.

"You have the right to an attorney," the Ghost of Sam Steele finished up. "And you have the right to a box full of Band-Aids and it looks to me like you might actually need them."

And looking down at Raven I am pretty sure that he did.

Chapter Forty – The Long Arm of the Storyteller

"That great big purple dog came and he fetched me here," the Ghost of Sam Steele explained. "He showed up in my office and he took me by the arm and he dragged me – which felt awfully peculiar. I didn't think that anything on earth could drag a ghost like that."

"I guess Death Dogs can do that sort of thing if they want to," I said as I leaned over and casually skritched the back of Old Shuck's ears. "As surprising as that might seem."

"You want to talk about surprising," Sam Steele's Ghost went on. "You should have been there when that big purple mutt hauled old Stony Britches down from off of his perch. "

I tried to picture Old Shuck hauling Nann Bijou from off of his Thunder Bay roost. As big as Old Shuck was he still stood about as tall as a good-sized chipmunk standing next to that big old Sleeping Mountain.

I looked at Old Shuck leaning happily against me, his big old purple tongue hanging out like a big fat rubber superhero cape left out on the clothesline in the rain.

I guess Old Shuck's bite was a WHOLE lot worse than his bark was.

"I let him get away with it," Nanna Bijou said. "I could have stopped him if I had honestly wanted to."

"Sure you could have," the Ghost of Sam Steele said sarcastically. "And if that big purple death mutt could talk I fully expect that he would tell you just how truly grateful he was for your show of sportsmanlike mercy."

"In case you haven't noticed," Nanna Bijou pointed out. "It is me who has actually apprehended our prisoner – unless you really expect me to believe that you were covering him while lying flat on your back."

Raven wasn't saying anything.

He was just lying there in Nanna Bijou's mighty stone grip – not moving so much as a single inch. He might as well have been a shadow of a rock, cast upon another rock for all of the movement he was doing.

"So is he my Dad?" I asked.

"He is one of them," Bigfoot said. "He isn't the one that really counts but he did marry your Mother and he did go off and leave her to raise you alone."

"So why did he ever even bother marrying my Mom if he didn't really want to stick around?" I asked.

Bigfoot shrugged.

"Well," Bigfoot said, with a shrug. "It might be that he had a plan. He is the original Trickster, after all. Remember, all of that energy that you were investing in believing in his myth fed him an awful lot of power."

"So you're saying that because I believed in him it made him stronger?" I said. "Is that what this was all about?"

I was gob-smacked by the thought.

He was my Dad, after all.

"So he was evil," I said.

"I wouldn't say evil," Bigfoot answered. "It might be that he wasn't really thinking about personal gain at all. It might be that he had told your Mother a love story so very strong that he began to believe in it himself. It might be the thought of actually committing to any one person that way scared him off."

I looked at Raven.

At my Dad.

He didn't even seem to see me.

All I could see were those eyes of his – just as cold and as black and implacable as a pair of tumbled stones fished out of a roaring northern river.

It was like he didn't even care.

"So what will happen to him?" I asked.

"We have a place in the mountains for him," Bigfoot explained.

"Like a jail?"

"Like a place where he can think about what he has done."

"Will that cure him?" I asked.

"There's nothing wrong with him to cure," Bigfoot said. "You can't cure a Trickster of being tricky any more than you can cure the wind from blowing."

"That doesn't seem like it will do much good at all."

"Well it won't hurt," Bigfoot said. "As a matter of fact I don't even think we will be able to keep him for all that long."

"He has a really good lawyer?" I asked, thinking of all of those law stories that I had seen on television.

Bigfoot just laughed.

"What's so funny?" I asked.

"Thinking that Raven needs a lawyer is what's so funny," Bigfoot explained. "That old bird knows more tricks than a thousand years of law school could ever teach. In fact, I am pretty sure that Raven actually INVENTED lawyers in the first place. It just seems like something that he would do."

I thought about that.

"No," Bigfoot went on. "I expect that he is already figuring some way of escaping. I'm surprised we've held him for as long as we have managed to."

That made me mad.

"So he gets away with it?" I said.

"He gets away with what?" Bigfoot asked.

"He gets away with hurting me and my Mom," I said. "He gets away with hurting Warren and hurting you and hurting everybody that I know."

Bigfoot just shook his head.

"You can't cure a hurtful nature unless it is your own nature to begin with," Bigfoot said. "Besides that he didn't kill you, did he?"

"No," I said.

"You grew up, didn't you?"

"I'm working on that," I said. "At seventeen I figure that I've got a little time left yet."

"Not more than a blink of eye when you are a part of a story," Bigfoot said. "How many sentences does it take to say that a man was born and lived and died?"

I thought about that.

"But I'm not a story," I said. "I am a real living person."

"Sure you are," Bigfoot agreed. "But we are all stories from cradle to the grave and it is up to us to tell our stories in the very best way that we can. That's what Raven gave you – when it comes down to it. He gave you a whole lot of story to tell."

I thought about that too.

"So what story are you going to tell?" Bigfoot asked.

I smiled at that.

I had figured things out.

I sat down beside the Warren cocoon and I grinned at it.

I could picture Warren standing there beside me with his big gorky Adam's apple frog-swallowing with happiness.

"Let me tell you about my stepdad," I said. "His name was Warren Teller and I am going to tell it to you."

I touched the cocoon and I felt something stir.

The End

ABOUT THE AUTHOR

Steve Vernon is a storyteller. The man was born with a campfire burning at his feet. The word "boring" does not exist in this man's vocabulary - unless he's maybe talking about termites or ice augers.

That's all that Steve Vernon will say about himself – on account of Steve Vernon abso-freaking HATES talking about himself in the third person.

But I'll tell you what.

If you LIKED the book that you just read drop me a Tweet on Twitter – @StephenVernon - and yes, old farts like me ACTUALLY do know how to twitter – and let me know how you liked the book – and I'd be truly grateful.

If you feel strongly enough to write a review, that's fine too. Reviews are ALWAYS appreciated – but I know that not all of you folks are into writing big long funky old reviews – so just shout the book out just any way that you can – because I can use ALL the help I can get.

Finally – if you enjoyed this novel you REALLY ought to hunt up BIGFOOT TRACKS – a three story collection of Creep Squad stories. And you also will want to keep an eye out for my next book in the Bigfoot saga – which I am calling WRESTLING BIGFOOT.

Ding-ding!

Also By Steve Vernon

My Regional Books – from Nimbus Publishing
Haunted Harbours: Ghost Stories from Old Nova Scotia
Wicked Woods: Ghost Stories from Old New Brunswick
Halifax Haunts: Exploring the City's Spookiest Spaces
Maritime Monsters: A Field Guide
The Lunenburg Werewolf and Other Stories of the Supernatural
Sinking Deeper OR My Questionable (Possibly Heroic) Decision to Invent a
Sea Monster
Maritime Murder: Deadly Crimes From the Buried Past

My E-Books

In the Dark and the Deep – Steve Vernon's Sea Tales #1
Harry's Mermaid – Steve Vernon's Sea Tales #2
I Know Why The Waters Of The Sea Taste of Salt – Steve Vernon's Sea Tales
#3
Flash Virus
Fighting Words
Tatterdemon
Devil Tree
Gypsy Blood
The Weird Ones
Two Fisted Nasty
Nothing to Lose –Adventures of Captain Nothing, Volume 1
Nothing Down – Adventures of Captain Nothing, Volume 2
Roadside Ghosts
Long Horn, Big Shaggy

And a whole lot more that I am just too lazy to list.

www.ingramcontent.com/pod-product-compliance
Lightning Source LLC
Chambersburg PA
CBHW050729180626
46814CB00002B/669

9 781927 765289